The Hero Laughs While Walking the Path of VENGEANCE a Second Time

2

SHURIA

EUMIS ELMIA

MINNALIS

"I really...
don't want
anyone to
ever see
me in this
miserable
state."

KAITO UKEI

Lagonid Beastfolk
MINNALIS

Hero
KAITO UKEI

← Partners in Crime →

Wants Revenge on ↓

Wants Revenge on ↓

Bigoted Village Girl
LUCIA

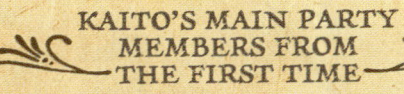

KAITO'S MAIN PARTY MEMBERS FROM THE FIRST TIME

← Sisters →

Spellcaster
EUMIS

Princess
ALICIA

Bearer of Scarlet Eyes
SHURIA

Merchant
GROND

Priestess
METELIA

The HeroLaughs While Walking the Path of VENGEANCE a Second Time

2 The Mad Spellcaster

NERO KIZUKA

Illustration by SINSORA

YEN ON

NEW YORK

The Hero Laughs While Walking the Path of VENGEANCE a Second Time

2

NERO KIZUKA

TRANSLATION BY JAKE HUMPHREY • COVER ART BY SINSORA

NIDOME NO YUSHA WA FUKUSYU NO MICHI O WARAI AYUMU Vol. 2
YUMEGURUI NO MAJUTSUSHI
©Kizuka Nero 2016
First published in Japan in 2016 by KADOKAWA CORPORATION, Tokyo.
English translation rights arranged with KADOKAWA CORPORATION, Tokyo,
through TUTTLE-MORI AGENCY, INC., Tokyo.

Yen On
150 W 30th Street, 19th Floor
New York, NY 10001

Visit us at yenpress.com • facebook.com/yenpress • twitter.com/yenpress
yenpress.tumblr.com • instagram.com/yenpress

First Yen On Edition: April 2022

Yen On is an imprint of Yen Press, LLC.
The Yen On name and logo are trademarks of Yen Press, LLC.

The publisher is not responsible for websites (or their content) that are not owned by the publisher.

Library of Congress Cataloging-in-Publication Data
Names: Kizuka, Nero, author. | Sinsora, illustrator. | Humphrey, Jake, translator.
Title: The hero laughs while walking the path of vengeance a second time /
Nero Kizuka ; illustration by Sinsora ; translation by Jake Humphrey.
Other titles: Nidome no yusha wa fukushuu no michi wo warai ayumu. English
Description: First Yen On edition. | New York, NY : Yen On, 2021.
Identifiers: LCCN 2021038196 | ISBN 9781975323707 (v. 1 ; trade paperback) |
ISBN 9781975323721 (v. 2 ; trade paperback)
Subjects: LCGFT: Fantasy fiction. | Light novels.
Classification: LCC PL872.5.I97 N5313 2021 | DDC 895.63/6—dc23
LC record available at https://lccn.loc.gov/2021038196

ISBNs: 978-1-9753-2372-1 (paperback)
978-1-9753-2373-8 (ebook)

1 3 5 7 9 10 8 6 4 2

LSC-C

Printed in the United States of America

2 The Mad Spellcaster

The Hero Laughs While Walking the Path of VENGEANCE a Second Time

NERO KIZUKA

CONTENTS

"What do you think? Are your lives really enough to tip the scales in my heart?"

"Eumis is **amazing**! She's hardworking and **kind,** and she saved Shelmie's life!"

PROLOGUE

How much value do my memories add to the scales in my heart?

There was nothing special about a certain place, per se. The important thing was the memories I made there, and nobody can ever take those away from me. They are the precious treasures from my first attempt at life.

...That's why I feel like they've now been sullied by dirty hands.

I know you weren't aware what that place meant to me. And I know you never thought critically about it. But to me, that transgression is more than enough to want you dead.

What do you think?

What do you think in a world like this, where you don't need a reason to bring death upon someone?

*   *   *

Where yesterday's friends could very easily become tomorrow's enemies?

In a world mired in filth and despair?

What do you think?

...Are your lives really enough to tip the scales in my heart?

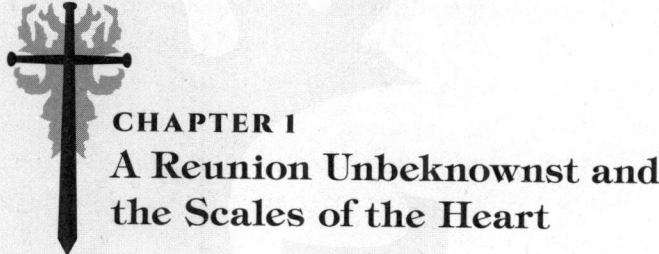

CHAPTER 1
A Reunion Unbeknownst and the Scales of the Heart

It had been several days since we'd left the capital. The road ahead stretched on forever. The only thing that had changed was that the sparse forests around us were turning gradually into denser woodlands.

"Ahhh... I knew it. It's too late for me," I said with a sigh.

"Hmm? What is?" asked Minnalis.

"Oh," I replied. "I mean I'm never going to feel safe walking down the middle of the road in broad daylight without a disguise or anything."

During my first life, my travels across the land had never gone this smoothly, especially not after the princess started sending people to assassinate me. I usually traveled at night to take full advantage of the Clothes of Dark Spirits, then either used all my mana and concentration to conceal my presence with my soul blades or used the Contrarian's Blade of Mirrors to alter my appearance. I rarely opted for the latter method, though, because there was only one form I could adopt, that of a pretty young girl, which wasn't ideal for lying low.

Of course, few people realized it was me in that form, if they even saw me at all. Still, it was better not to attract attention whenever possible, and besides, that was without factoring in the repulsive men who I drew in with that guise.

"So you see," I explained, "I avoided the road during daytime, and if I had to go somewhere, I'd wear a hood and blend in with a traveling caravan so nobody would recognize me."

What a miserable life of traveling, if you could even call randomly fleeing "travel."

"To be honest, it doesn't even feel right hanging out with you. Even when I mingled with the caravans, I never conversed or interacted with anyone else."

I wasn't trying to insult her. It was just that traveling alone had been my life for so long, it was going to take some time to readjust.

"But what's that got to do with it being too late?" Minnalis asked, confused.

"I just mean I feel like I've had to live like a criminal my whole life, always anxious when out under the heavens."

It wasn't even as if I'd done anything to be ashamed of. My parents always told me to hold my head up high for the Sun Deity, and now I couldn't even do that. It was a small promise in the grand scheme of things, but it was another one I'd broken.

Well, I suppose I'm probably a lost cause anyway, given I'm planning on torturing and killing all my old friends.

"The heavens?" asked Minnalis.

"Oh, I guess that sounds weird 'cause you guys don't worship the sun and the sky here," I mused.

Maybe there *was* some cult somewhere that deified the sun if I looked hard enough, but it seemed like no major religion did, at least to my knowledge. The religions of this land venerated either God himself, or something known as "the Spirits." Though moral priorities differed slightly, that was pretty much the only difference.

"In my old land, we believed the sun was a god. If you did something bad, then you were supposed to feel guilty about showing yourself before it."

"Huh. What a strange belief."

"Yeah. In fact, it wasn't just the sun. In my country, they said that gods dwelled inside all sorts of things, like tools. It was inconsistent for sure."

I mean, I could see the good in that belief, but it was certainly very bold of us to decide that gods would deign to take up residence in our old pots and pans. Anyway, I wasn't sure how to reconcile this with the fact that I knew a god, or rather, a goddess. At least, that's what she called herself.

"Whatever, I'm sure I'll get used to it soon enough. You don't need to worry about anything."

Humans are an adaptive species. Just as traveling alone had become a habit, journeying with Minnalis would surely become one, too. And in any case, I don't intend to let ethics cloud my judgment. I've learned the hard way just how big of a mistake that can be. Besides, I think pretty much everyone would agree I'm on the path of evil now.

"Let's change the subject," I said, stopping in my tracks. "Here's the first lesson of the day."

"Hmm?!"

Minnalis's ears perked up, and her face became deathly serious. To spice up our travels, I'd taken to engaging in a training of sorts to increase her base stats. She knew this meant another lesson was about to begin.

"There's a fine target around here somewhere. Find out where. You'll never uncover it relying solely on your physical senses. Its camouflage and stealth abilities are off the charts," I clarified when I saw her nose twitching.

Her approach wasn't a bad one. As a beastfolk, her physical abilities were higher than those of humans, and that extended to her senses as well. Tracking via smell was second nature to her, but we couldn't let it stay that way. Get dependent on a single method, and you'll be screwed when you face an enemy that it doesn't work on.

Having strengths and weaknesses is only natural, but if you allow a strength to be defeated, or a weakness to go unmitigated, it could cost you your life. That's something an enemy could take advantage of.

"Monsters can't hide their mana," I hinted. "You should be able to pick up on those traces and then track it like you normally would."

Is this too advanced for her right now?

The creature wasn't impossible to find; I had just done it myself. I'd been scanning the area, looking for something that could serve as Minnalis's target, the whole time we were walking.

It's hard to explain what sensing magic feels like. It's like straining to see through a dense fog, or trying to pick out a single voice from indistinct mumbles coming through a wall. Sometimes, it's like trying to grab mist. And because it was so hard to put into words, practical experience was of the utmost importance.

"The monster shouldn't be so hard to defeat once you find it, and its meat is pretty tasty. I think we'll have it for lunch."

Despite appearances, it was delicious. Plus, in this day and age, even food products in Japan are genetically modified. If something could be done about the way it *looked*, then perhaps it could earn a coveted S rank on my monster meat tier list.

"Oh! I found it! It's over there!" cried Minnalis.

"Greeeeee!!"

Fwip. Minnalis's throwing knife flew toward the base of a tree. From seemingly out of thin air, a large frog, about the size of a boar, began materializing into view. It was a Pelia Grok, a mutated variant of a much smaller species known as a Pure Grok.

"I-is this thing really edible, Master?"

Since coming here, I had been subjected to all kinds of weird and wonderful cuisines and eaten things that would make any normal high schooler turn up their nose. Now I could handle just about anything, as long as it wasn't insects. So it wasn't because our target was a frog that Minnalis reacted the way she did. There was some other visual element that shocked her.

"You're saying that because of its color, right?"

It was not a friendly-looking color. Its slimy body was purple and green, with red and black patches. Warts covered its body, and its flabby pink tongue lolled from its mouth. Its appearance just screamed "I'm poisonous! Don't eat me!" I don't know how the first person discovered this creature was edible, but I commend their courage.

"Well, I can vouch for its taste; I've had it myself. I can guarantee it's at least two ranks above what we've been eating so far."

As long as I had good food in my belly, I could forgive the other hardships of travel. I couldn't wait to finally sink my teeth into some juicy meat. The forests around the capital were cleared out by the royal knights on the regular, so only the weakest, most common enemies like goblins, garm, and boars could be found there. And I'm sorry to say that the meat on those enemies left much to be desired. Barely any parts of goblins and garm were even edible. I'd heard of one land where goblin testicles were considered a delicacy, but I wasn't interested in trying that myself.

So I guess we found something besides insects I won't eat, then.

"Is that right, Master? In that case, I'm looking forward to it," said Minnalis, sounding a little excited.

"Well, we'll just sprinkle some salt on it and spit roast it. We've had nothing lately but soup." I walked over to the Pelia Grok and lifted it up by the legs. Its body was coated in slime, and it was cold to the touch. "Minnalis, there's a trick to preparing this. I'll show you. Could you get the table?"

"Of course, Master."

Minnalis set up a large, kidney-shaped table she pulled from her rucksack. Before being enslaved, Minnalis had always cooked for her ailing mother. It was an insult to even compare her skills in the kitchen with those of a casual cook like me.

"Hmm, now that I'm getting a good look at it, it is a bit slipshod."

The table's construction was far from perfect. It was little more than a cross section of a large tree with some legs attached. I'd improvised it so that Minnalis would have *something* to work with, but it was clearly unfinished. Granted, the table was perfectly smooth and solid as a rock thanks to my S-rank abilities, but you couldn't change the fact that it was just untreated wood. It wasn't waterproof or varnished, so it would rot with time.

"We'll buy a real table when we get to Elmia," I assured her.

"What? But, Master, you put so much effort into making this one for us..."

"That's fine; this was only supposed to be temporary, anyway."

After rubbing some salt into the body of the Pelia Grok, I used the Fairy's Blade of Water to wash away the slime. Then, slicing open its back with my knife, I separated the meat, bones, and giblets.

"That should do it. Can I leave the rest of the cooking to you?" I asked.

"Of course, Master."

I handed her the skewers I had made from a few branches and left her to set about preparing the large cuts. By the time I had finished wiping down the table, I could smell the salted meat slowly roasting over the fire.

"Mmm, that smells good."

"They'll be done soon, Master. Give me a minute."

Minnalis had taken care of most of the process. I suppose that wasn't such a bad thing, since the finished product would turn out better this way.

"Sounds good." I sat down on the ground across the bonfire from her. The crackle of fat as it fell into the fire set my stomach growling. "Mmm, are you sure it's not done yet...?"

"No. Frog meat has to be cooked a little longer," she snapped back, a serious glint in her eyes.

"O-oh."

Just then, I sensed something else nearby.

...I guess the scent of cooked meat must have attracted it.

But then what popped out of the bushes was a small garm pup. Just as Minnalis was about to toss a knife at it, I stopped her. "Hold on."

"Huh? Master?"

"It's not hostile... I think it's just hungry. It looks like it hurt its leg and can't hunt."

I took a piece of uncooked meat and tossed it over to the garm. The monster poked it a few times with its front paw, before tearing into it viciously.

"Oh, you're a hungry little fella. Wait there, I'll fix up your leg for you."

Trying not to frighten it, I conjured up the Nephrite Blade of Verdure behind my back and cured the garm's wound while it was distracted by the food.

"Should you be doing that, Master?" asked Minnalis.

"I wouldn't kill a baby dog just for the experience points, even if it *is* a monster."

I doubted the creature understood what I'd been saying, but still it gave me a lick as if in thanks.

"Now you've had your food, shoo. This is human territory. It's not safe for a little one like you."

The pup looked a little bewildered as I tried to shoo it away, before turning and fleeing into the depths of the forest.

"...Weren't you going to keep it?" asked Minnalis. "I thought that's why you helped it..."

"No," I said. "That was...just on a whim."

That's right, it was just on a whim.

A whimsical favor to the garm cub I'd condemned *during my last life*. I saved this one because it pained me to see it die and do nothing to help.

"I befriended a garm pup once before. But it ended up dying because of me."

This whelp, weak and hungry, had reminded me of that creature. I couldn't just do nothing. Even though I knew that the two garm had nothing to do with each other.

"It was just an impulse. There's no significance to it whatsoever." I turned back toward the fire and reached out for a bite to eat.

"Master, it's not ready yet."

"...Fine," I relented, my arm dropping dejectedly by my side. "I'll wait."

We trekked a bit farther that night and found somewhere suitable to set up camp. Lying beside the fire, Minnalis turned over beneath her blanket. I was tired, too, but on the road, you never knew when monsters could strike. What's more, we were a party of only two. It would be easy for a pack of monsters to attack us, especially after sunset.

I used to put up barriers while I was sleeping during my fugitive days, so I'd never needed to worry about keeping watch. Now, however, I had way too little MP, so there was simply no way I could keep a strong enough barrier active until morning.

I brought a tea of medicinal herbs to my lips.

"Ow! My tongue..."

I grimaced. The drink was just hot enough not to burn me, while the heat and bitterness kept me awake. It was made from fuzzyweed, a wonderful fantasy plant that eased drowsiness and fought off exhaustion. It grew almost everywhere and was incredibly cheap, even in the cities, so it was a powerful friend to beginner adventurers everywhere. The problem was it tasted like pure cocoa and coffee and matcha mixed together, and you had to brew it right after sundown and drink it immediately, while the water was still piping hot, or else it lost its effects. It was a cruel prank of a drink, but my only other options were to buy expensive magic items for setting up a barrier, hire a wizard to do it for me, or travel as part of a larger party and set up a proper watch order. In fact, this was one of the original reasons I'd gone after a slave—before I found Minnalis, my partner in crime, that is. As long as you could put up with the taste and heat, fuzzyweed allowed you to travel with a party of only two people. That meant it was always in demand.

My shift ran from sundown to midnight, while Minnalis watched the camp until sunrise. I glanced at the hourglass marking the length of my shift. There was still a lot of sand in the top. It looked like it would be several more hours before I could drift off.

"Hurgh… It's so bitter…," I said under my breath. I didn't want to wake Minnalis, but I just had to complain to someone, even if that was just myself. The fire crackled. I added some sticks to keep it from going out, then put down my wooden cup, and watched the flickering flames. It was a good time to sort through some things in my head.

The first thing that came to mind was the incident at the walls of the capital.

I had to stop focusing on people who had nothing to do with my revenge. This was important; if I didn't draw a line, the boundaries of my revenge would blur. It would mean that I wasn't confident enough in my conviction.

When is it revenge, and when is it just taking out my anger?

If I left that line undefined, eventually, like a poison, it would lead to doubt. And if that doubt went unchecked, I would soon become nothing more than a monster, destroying anyone and everyone in my path.

Revenge is an emotion.

We set out on the path of vengeance to prevent that feeling from destroying us. If we gave in to it and let the heat inside us take control, it would never extinguish, not even long after putting all our foes to death.

It would break us completely. We'd never be human again… At that point, we may as well be dead.

So I wouldn't cross this line I drew. Since I didn't want to lose myself to hate, the only people I should plan to exact my vengeance upon were those directly connected to me. It was going to be impossible to prevent some unrelated parties from getting caught in the cross fire, though, and that, I had no problem with. I wouldn't stay my blade if it brought me closer to taking out my true foes or if it was necessary for my survival. Any hesitation I had on that front had died long ago, before I did, on the road of my previous journey.

The important word was balance. Fail to control the anger in my heart, and I'd lose myself to destruction. But try too hard to save everybody, and I'd spread my efforts too thin and lose it all.

That's why I'd stopped using good and evil as a basis for my decisions.

"It's not the whole world I swore revenge on. There's no point in torturing people who have nothing to do with me."

I said it aloud, gave those thoughts form, so that I wouldn't forget it. That's right. It's not the whole world. I swore revenge on my old comrades. They're the ones who double-crossed me.

I had already misjudged who my enemies were the first time around. I would not make the same mistake twice.

"Oh, how much easier it would be if I really did hate the world…"

Things would have been much easier. I wouldn't have had to be selective; I could just run around slaughtering whatever I came across. That's probably what I would have done if I'd never met Leticia. If all that ever mattered to me was getting back to my world.

When I first came here, it didn't feel real. A world of stats and levels, of magic and skills. Ferocious monsters of all shapes and sizes that gave you experience when you killed them, allowing you to reach superhuman levels of power. Potions and magic that could heal wounds, even regrow lost limbs. It was like I'd been trapped in a game. One where all I had to do was defeat evil and restore peace to the land.

If I'd been betrayed without ever realizing this world actually was real, I probably would have seen the people of this land as nothing more than tools. I could easily imagine what I would look like then. A monster, joylessly executing my retribution until the entire world ended up consumed in flames.

I'm sure it would be very easy. But it would also give me no delight, no satisfaction. It would amount to little more than a senseless act of self-destruction; a dramatic suicide.

"Crap."

The bonfire collapsed, bringing me out of my reverie. It had gotten quite cold now, and I hurriedly threw on another few dry-looking twigs.

"…Ugh. It's so bitter…"

My cup of fuzzyweed decoction was still pretty full. I took another sip and pulled out a handful of dried vegetables I had picked up in town to take away the bitterness.

Next, I took a fairly long branch in my hand and activated the Fairy's Blade of Water. Reforming it into a knifelike blade, I set about sharpening the stick to a point. I then stuck some of the dried vegetables to it, roasted them gently over the fire, added some seasonings, and sucked on them.

The night was still young.

"All right."

I could think about my troubles all I liked, but the answers wouldn't come out of thin air. I decided to change the subject, so I set about figuring out how to assign all the experience points I had gathered along the road since leaving the capital.

For starters, I paid off my debt in full and got myself a few points away from level 2. That way, I could level up quickly if need be. I had to think about when the best time for that would be, though, since I could boost my stats quite a lot just by unlocking soul blades. There was one that temporarily lowered my stats in exchange for an EXP boost, but it also reduced the attack of all other weapons to zero while it was equipped, so I was simply far too weak to use it until I got a little stronger.

After that, I had about 25,000 points remaining.

"Hmm... What should I do...?"

The enemies around these parts weren't bad in terms of experience, but the problem was they were hard to encounter. Since I planned to stay here in Elmia for a little while, there wouldn't be a lot of experience to go around.

And so it came to pass that despite a lot of head-racking and hand-wringing, I had left my experience points unallocated until now, prompting Minnalis to ask me, *"Master, are you a wuss?"* I wanted to cry. Not piss myself, though.

"I feel like Minnalis has gotten a lot stricter with me lately..."

While she still respected the master-slave relationship, it seemed like she sometimes had this aura about her I couldn't defy. Not that I was expecting her to serve my every whim, but something seemed off.

I let out a brief sigh and poked the fire, and my mind drifted toward the things that had happened along our journey. I had never really paid attention to the world around me last time. It didn't really matter to me so long as I had food to eat, and I didn't have time to go off exploring, anyway. So now, when I would buy some trinket of dubious utility or be taken in by the rip-off prices of the food stalls, Minnalis would look at me with that emotionless grin of hers and say, "*Master, are you an idiot?*" I suppose growing up in a poor village made her reluctant to waste money even when we could.

The only times she smiled genuinely were when she was coming up with new and exotic forms of revenge, putting them into practice against some random goblin she'd found, or occasionally, when she was in a good mood, getting MP-drunk and reveling in a brain-dead stupor all night.

In any case, it looked like I'd need to finally make up my mind and decide which soul blades to unlock. And so, after much umming and ahhing, I went with the Challenger's Blade of Adversity. My stats were going to be on the low side for a while, so there would be plenty of opportunities to use it, and if it turned out my opponents' stats were lower, then I could simply switch to another soul blade and avoid the penalty that way.

That had cost me 15,000 experience points, and so I was now sitting at 10,000. I considered unlocking a soul blade that would give me an Agility or MP buff, but I decided against it. If I used these experience points to level up, I could easily get to level 20. I could keep it in reserve so I'd have more leeway to adapt to whatever came my way.

"Let's leave it there," I announced, and when I looked over at the hourglass, the top half was completely empty. That had taken longer than I'd thought. I moved to wake Minnalis, but she sat up in bed before I even reached her.

"Master, it's time for us to switch," she told me.

"Oh, you're already awake."

"Yes......Master, you sure like muttering to yourself."

"Wha—?!"

Well, that's unavoidable, isn't it? I've been traveling solo for so long. It's like when you live by yourself!

"I don't mind it during the day, but at night, it's hard to sleep because I want to know what you're talking about."

Her poker face I could probably chalk up to that skill of hers. That meant she was probably pretty angry at me.

"I-I'm sorry..."

"No need to apologize, just keep it in mind in the future."

I meekly pulled up my blanket and closed my eyes. It was starting to feel like the balance of power in our relationship was shifting. She would go along with my plans and decisions, as long as she didn't have any serious objections, but apart from that... Well, it wasn't as though I didn't even exist to her. It was more like she was concerned about me, but she expressed that sentiment pretty coldly.

The reason for this behavior was obvious. She didn't like that I'd put myself in danger back at the capital.

Beneath her exterior, Minnalis seemed a lot more serious than me. I knew I shouldn't read too much into it, but it did make me wonder...

My head filled with such thoughts, I gently drifted off to sleep.

"Looks like you're fast asleep, Master."

After making sure he wouldn't wake up, I turned off my "Iron Mask" skill and set about combing his hair like usual.

"Ahhh, how is Master's voice so pleasing to my ears? Has he the blood of a siren in his veins?"

I struggled to keep my voice low. My face, unfettered by the skill I had been previously using, melted into one of pure pleasure.

"I need to buy some sort of magic item that can record his voice and preserve it for all eternity..."

No, that's not a waste of our money. It would be a perfectly sensible purchase... And this is totally unrelated, but I suppose I'll keep my mouth shut the next time Master wants to buy some useless trinket at the market. Perhaps I could gently coax him into heading somewhere I can find a magic item like that the next time we're in town.

It's just the snacking I can't forgive...

I always made my displeasure known whenever Master dropped his coin at a food stall. It was *my* job to cook for him, and no one else's. I get the ingredients more cheaply and make sure they're worthy of his plate. And after all that, he has the nerve to say to me "Oh no, I'll get something in town, it's fine."

Oh, what am I saying? My food is nowhere near being fit for his palate. I must improve. "The way to a man's heart is through his stomach" is apparently what they say. I'll make sure he doesn't develop a gut for anyone else but me.

"...But I wish he wouldn't use disposable cutlery. What a waste. Oh well. I suppose I'll have to study the bars and taverns to learn what he likes. The food stalls, on the other hand, are a little suspicious. Who knows what they put in their food...?"

I spoke quietly so that even if Master were to wake up, he wouldn't be able to hear me. I suppose I've become more like him, talking to myself in the middle of the night. What a pleasant thought. But since I just told him off for the same thing, it'd be best if he didn't catch me doing it.

I continued to tend the bonfire, turning those frivolous musings over in my head, and soon enough the night broke into dawn.

We continued on our journey, engaging in lively debate about the finer methods of torture, and training ourselves for when we could put those methods into practice, until we eventually arrived at the town of Golet. Our next destination was Elmia, but between us and it lay a vast forest.

We'd found an inn rumored to have good lodgings and rested to ease our weariness. While the bedding wasn't as soft as the stories had made them out to be, it was still a good-quality inn and a lucky find. There's nothing better than down duvets and mattresses stuffed with cotton rather than straw.

"Good morning, Master."

"Mrph... I'm so sleepy... Five more minutes..."

Lucking out was rare. As tourists, we couldn't exactly expect to get the best information by asking around, and even though I retained memories from my previous life, rating every single lodging in the land was not exactly high on my list of priorities.

That was why I wanted to sink into softness for as long as I could.

"Just let me stay a little longer...," I mumbled, pulling the soft duvet over my head.

"We have to be up early today! Didn't you want to go to the Adventurers Guild?" snapped Minnalis, cruelly stripping me of my heavenly fleece.

"Nooooo... Give it back..."

"No. This is mine now—I mean... Never mind, just get up."

Minnalis tossed the blanket onto her own bed. Then she came for my pillows. Bit by bit, I was robbed of my dear bedding, and when still I clung reluctantly to the bare sheets, she grabbed the side of the bed and lifted it sharply using her beastfolk strength, rolling me out and onto the floor.

"Aaaagh! Owww!"

Unfortunately, I could do nothing with the hard ground, and so at last I stood up and confronted the demon in my room.

"You don't have to be so violent, Minnalis!"

"I'm sorry, Master, but you've already slept in once!"

...Did I? Hmm, come to think of it, perhaps I did say "Five more minutes" five minutes ago as well...

"Besides," she went on, "you told me to make sure you woke up this time."

"Did I? Huh, so I did."

As my mind cleared, the memory of what I'd said last night returned to me. I hadn't wanted to oversleep again like I had done in the capital.

There was *a particular reason* I needed to be up early today. That was why we'd bought a double room. Well, one reason, anyway. The other was Minnalis.

"Can you really not stand to be in the same room as me, Master?

"Oh, I see, sometimes boys have to be alone.

"It's fine, I totally understand."

...Minnalis had said, with reproachful eyes that proved she didn't understand, but it shook me so much I agreed to take a double anyway. Now that I thought about it, though, I bet that only made me look even more guilty.

...No, she really did have the wrong impression.

"I already asked the kitchen to make us breakfast while you were sleeping in, so let's go downstairs."

"Good idea, let's get some grub."

I put a lid on the troubling thoughts that were beginning to surface and expelled the last of the drowsiness from my body with a terrible yawn that seemed to contain all the darkness of my worst nightmares.

Then I got dressed and went downstairs.

I made sure we each waited in the corridor while the other was changing. Minnalis suggested we just do it together to save time, but I would die on this hill. I mean, men, you know what it's like in the morning, right? Just being in the same room was hard enough. Er, so to speak.

As we feasted on the breakfast provided by the inn, we exchanged our ideas on torture.

"I still think being slowly devoured alive is the worst way to go."

"You do seem to be partial to that one, Minnalis. For me, it's less about the death and more about seeing them suffer. Some people have low pain tolerances, while others don't feel it at all. There would be no point torturing the latter with physical wounds. They could die before they even realized what was happening, and then it's game over."

"Good point, Master. We want them to expire in misery and regret. To see their faces warped with..."

Of course, we were careful not to let anyone nearby hear what we were talking about. Minnalis wasn't currently hiding her ears and tail, and her rabbit ears flopped around as she spoke. I had told her to stop concealing them around the time we passed through Dotre.

Beastfolk were oppressed in the Orollea Kingdom, but it wasn't as if everyone in the country hated them. In fact, beastfolk adventurers traveled through towns and villages outside the capital all the time. They had full citizenship and were treated just like anyone else. The only people who despised them were the nobility in the capital. Most of them had never even seen a beastfolk before and just assumed they were an inferior species.

That was why beastfolk were treated so badly in the capital and why there was such a bustling black market trade for them; curious aristocrats wanted to purchase one without anybody finding out.

In that sense, Minnalis had been quite unlucky. Perhaps the village she'd grown up in had been an isolated settlement of bigots. There were even some in our current town. Not a lot, but some.

I suppose I had been staring at her for a while, as she asked, "...Are you worried, Master? About my ears?"

"Hmm? I think they're fine," I said. "They're pretty cute. You look good."

Even those who discriminated against beastfolk would find Minnalis quite beautiful. In fact, this world was full of gorgeous people compared to ours, and yet even among them, she stood out as the cream of the crop. She could give my little sister a run for her money.

Around these parts, there was almost no prejudice against beastfolk, and the odd merchant or adventurer would give Minnalis a passing glance, before noticing the Slave Brand on her neck and leering at me. When that happened, a frigid glare from Minnalis was often enough to send them packing. And if those men happened to be with women of their own, the aftermath was always a riot to watch.

"O-okay. Um... Are we going to the Adventurers Guild today?"

"Mm, yeah. We're quite far from the capital now. It's only a little farther to Elmia."

Word of our deeds wouldn't have traveled this far out, and we needed the status and privileges that being a recognized adventurer bestowed. As a hero, I'd had access to those benefits the first time around without even having to lift a finger, but now I was going to build it all up again myself. The top-ranked adventurers received some very nice perks, but I couldn't afford to rise through the ranks too quickly, or I'd draw unwanted attention. It was quite the conundrum.

Well, we'd cross that bridge when we came to it. First things first, I needed to register and get my foot in the door.

"Hmm...this breakfast is just all right..."

The portions were large enough, and it wasn't totally inedible, but there was a quality to the mouthfeel I couldn't quite describe. Honestly, Minnalis's cooking was leagues above this mush.

"I agree, Master. I was wondering why this place wasn't more popular. It's cheap, and the beds are good… Now I know."

She took another bite of her food and pulled a face very difficult to put into words.

We'll pick something up in town for supper.

After taking care of breakfast, we set out a little earlier in the day than usual. Our destination was the Adventurers Guild. Our mission, to register me as a member.

The guild connected adventurers with people who needed things done. It existed in every country and was a completely neutral institution founded on the tenets of freedom, power, and exploration. It guaranteed recognition for its members and moderated disputes between them and their clients. In other words, it was a freelancer agency for people with swords.

Now, the word *adventurer* had quite a ring to it, but the actual job wasn't so glamorous. Gathering herbs, picking up trash, collecting rent, investigating cheating spouses, smuggling letters, and escort duty were the kinds of odd jobs you were expected to do, and unless you had a contract, you'd likely never work for the same client twice. Work was unsteady and irregular, so your income and lifestyle as an adventurer were constantly in flux.

That said, you only had to deal with those sorts of tasks when starting out. An adventurer's primary task was the slaying of monsters and the collection of their materials. Once you leveled up enough by killing goblins and garm, you got to the point where you could start raking in the dough by taking on stronger monsters. Of course, they wouldn't send you into battle against the most dangerous enemies right away. Adventurers were divided into categories based on their exploits, and you could only take on work that you were strong enough for.

Excluding the bottom rank of apprentices not yet old enough to become adventurers, who were sometimes called G rank, the lowest official one was F, and this was where you'd find your goblin- and garm-slayers. From here, you worked your way up the rungs by proving yourself, until eventually you could ascend to the highest rank of SSS. Similarly, all identified monsters were given a grade from F through SSS, sometimes appended with a plus or minus to indicate where they fell within that classification. It was this rank that determined whether an adventurer was suited for taking on a particular foe.

All this meant was that while you were a low rank, you saw a lot of danger, but didn't get any of the juicy jobs.

Adventurers who attained the title of SSS were regarded as legends. But only a small fraction could kill enough dragons and clear out enough dungeons to get that far. Most people either died in the attempt or found a level they were comfortable with and stayed put.

Still, the profession was in no risk of dying out so long as there were people looking to make a name for themselves, or who had no other avenue of employment. All you needed to become an adventurer was to be over fourteen years of age and able to pay the registration fee of a couple large silver coins—about the cost of a single meal.

You didn't need connections or riches; no distinguished career or birth. You could even take the fee on credit if you had no money at all, so even an orphan bereft of worldly possessions could become one.

For that reason, adventuring was also seen as an occupation for those who couldn't find safe and stable employment, or as a home for people who rejected that lifestyle.

Now, getting back to the point, scoring an adventurer's ID papers for ourselves would come with many benefits. First, and perhaps this went without saying, we could prove our identity. The four powers that ruled this continent were the kingdom, land of human supremacy; the beast lands, land of beastfolk supremacy; the empire, a meritocracy; and the Church. Lost in the cracks between these four titans were several smaller and mostly inconsequential nations. Having the status of an adventurer in good standing with the guild made traveling from one country to another much smoother. Citizens without status were not permitted to dawdle too long in large cities; a stay longer than ten days required a proof of character of some sort.

Second, adventurers were exempt from civic entry tax. In some ways, this was a no-brainer. If they had to pay every time they wanted to enter and leave a city, then their services would become prohibitively expensive.

And third, there was an unspoken rule that you didn't pry too closely into an adventurer's history.

There were nobles whose houses had fallen into ruin, ex-criminals who had put their old lives behind them, aristocrats and royalty seeking to hide their true identities. People who changed their names and took up a life on the road. Everyone knew you never asked questions about an adventurer's past. There were many in this line of work who preferred that such things remained secret forever.

It was perfect for a couple of fugitives like me and Minnalis. Well, I guess technically, that was just me.

The first and third points were what I was after. The second point was probably more what Minnalis was interested in.

"By the way, Master, how come we need to go to the guild so early in the morning?" asked Minnalis. The sun had not even fully risen, and many shops were still getting ready for business.

"Like I said, we want to avoid the clichés."

All sorts of things could happen when you signed up to be an adventurer. Some of the old hands start giving the new guy some trouble, one thing leads to another, and suddenly everyone's got a favor to ask of the guild's new rising star. I'm sure you've all seen it a dozen times before, and I have no intention of rehashing that old, worn-out trope. Besides, I had enough of being people's slave the first time around.

"We really don't want to get into a fight. For now, we just want to keep as low a profile as possible. That's why we're going in early, so that there won't be so many people."

"Huh.., I suppose I have heard of things like that happening…" Minnalis tilted her head, apparently unconvinced.

In the stories read in this world, upstart heroes would often run into their first major challenge while registering at the guild, so she definitely knew what I was getting at. She probably just thought I was acting overly cautious by expecting a fairy-tale-esque plot twist. Well, maybe I was. But only because it did, in fact, happen to me the first time around when I registered at the capital. Just one little fight was enough to land me in hot water with the guild leader, who saw me as "*having potential, but a little rough around the edges…*" You know how it goes. It was all because I'd needed some social standing besides that of a hero, and I had ended up with a lot more trouble on my plate that I didn't need.

Anyway, while I was remembering all that, I suddenly found myself standing before our destination. It was a wooden building that towered over its neighbors, with a sign hanging out front depicting the guild's crest: a sword and a shield marked with a wing.

"Nice, there are even fewer people around than I expected."

"…Does it really happen that often?"

Minnalis still had her doubts. She didn't get it.

She *just* didn't get it.

"Minnalis, it's like I'm hexed. Whenever I go to the slums, I get accosted by thugs. It's the curse of being an otherworlder. All we can do is be aware of it and try to avoid it."

"Right… I see. Sounds tough."

Minnalis obviously still didn't believe me, but she said nothing more than that. Listening to her, even I wondered if I was overthinking things. But it didn't matter, just so long as everything went smoothly. I walked through the doors with Minnalis by my side and approached the reception desk.

Inside, it was as I expected: not many adventurers had shown up yet. The area we were in was quite large, modeled on a tavern or a restaurant. The few people present already were squinting at the rather *sparse* pickings on the quest board.

That was typical for the early hours; the new quests were posted just after noon. Why noon, you ask? Well, because then the guild's tavern could make its money.

Quests were first come, first served, so to get the best jobs you would show up right after they were posted, and then perhaps you'd stick around and grab lunch at the tavern.

Many adventurers took advantage of their flexible working hours to wake up a little later, often skipping breakfast entirely and enjoying a big lunch instead. Though that was more of a time-management issue on their part and not really the guild's fault. Still, the system did little to discourage it.

"Let's see…"

After taking a brief glance around, I walked up to the reception desk. The whole thing was constructed out of plywood, with several booths where the receptionists sat. As for the receptionists themselves, they came in two flavors: pretty young women and hulking, great big oafs so strong they didn't look right sitting at a desk.

Because of their profession's low barrier to entry, many adventurers were uneducated, or rather, unversed in culture and etiquette. To them, might meant right. Not all adventurers were like this, and people tended to learn the importance of keeping good relations with others as they rose through the ranks. Unfortunately, those who did so were very much the minority, so some of the more *heavy-handed* receptionists were chosen specifically for their abilities to deal with those unruly sorts. The pretty ladies, of which there were a fair few, were there to counteract that. It wouldn't do to go scaring off all the freelancers. Besides, some of the more, shall we say, *inexperienced* adventurers responded better to a lovely face on the other side of the window.

I guess what I'm trying to say is that people are all idiots.

"Good morning! What can I do for you today?"

I headed to the second-closest desk and the woman there greeted me with a customer-winning smile. I could feel Minnalis's glare burning a hole in my back, but I didn't care. Why should I have to talk to some meathead this early in the morning? It's not like looks particularly mattered to me, but if I have the choice then I don't see why I have to speak to a guy who sucks all the air out of the room. I'm not into men.

"I'd like to sign us both up to be adventurers."

"Both of you?" The receptionist woman looked me up and down with an evaluating glance. It was too obvious. She must have been new.

"I'm sorry, but only people ages fourteen and older can register to become adventurers. Until then, you'll have to be an apprentice. You won't be able to raise your rank, but you'll be able to take on odd jobs around the city as long as they're safe. And while you won't be able to benefit from the adventurer perks, you can make free use of our special beginner training course, and—"

"Actually, I'm seventeen. And she's sixteen."

I hesitated in my response because I was actually over twenty. Or at least, it felt like it. My status screen said I was seventeen, so I guess I had to go with that.

"Huh?" The receptionist lady stared at me with wide-eyed shock.

It was a magnificent look of surprise, and one I was well used to by now. It was obvious she was taken aback by me specifically, and not just bad at judging ages. And of course, I wasn't trying to look young or anything. It was just the magic of being Japanese, I guess.

To be honest, I was going to think nothing of it until I looked over at Minnalis, who was wearing a totally straight face. I'm sure she was laughing at me until she activated her Iron Mask skill. I needed to talk to her about that later.

"Understood. Then could both of you touch this crystal, please?" she asked, producing a small sphere about the size of a baseball. It was a magic item known as an Age-Reading Orb, and as the name suggested, it could detect people's ages. I didn't know exactly how it worked, but it could tell if we were fourteen or not.

"This ball will turn red when you touch it if you're under fourteen. The age restriction is laid down jointly by all the nations, so we couldn't bend the rules even if we wanted to. Please understand."

I wasn't asking her to bend the rules for me. She must have assumed I was a noble or something. Probably because of Minnalis, or rather, the Slave Brand upon her neck. Slaves were expensive, and we were dressed in fairly fancy garb from the capital. It was clear we weren't exactly short of money.

So she was probably thinking, *This whelp is going to tell me he doesn't care what the Age-Reading Orb says, and that he can use his influence to get whatever he wants.*

In fact, the first time around, I had already seen someone try to do precisely that.

But even though I knew she was right to take precautions, it still annoyed me to be lumped in with those sorts of people. And even through her perfect smile, I could clearly see the disdain she held for me deep down. Minnalis must have noticed it, too, for she dispelled her Iron Mask and gave a slightly disapproving glare.

All right, calm down, me. This actually works to my advantage.

I should have expected we'd be scorned because we appeared so young. But that was actually a good thing. The whole idea was we didn't want to attract attention, and by concealing our true power, we'd succeeded at exactly that. Still didn't mean I had to like it, though.

I took the Age-Reading Orb in my hand and, sure enough, it turned green.

"Minnalis."

"Fine."

I tossed the orb to her, and it glowed green in her hand, too.

"Er... Apologies, but the orb is actually guild property, so please be careful with it...," cautioned the receptionist, a slight twitch in one eye. Looked like someone had put a stick up her butt. If she'd been placed on duty without any experience, though, then she must have been fairly capable. I considered intimidating her a bit to put her in her place, but I could easily imagine that turning into a whole kerfuffle with one of those meatheads standing in the corner, so I dismissed the idea.

"Ahhh, sorry. It just didn't look that valuable to me. I'll try to treat it with a little more respect than *the guild shows its adventurers.*"

"...Gh." She offered a pleasant smile, filled with poison.

It seemed she understood what I was really trying to say. *I know what you're up to, and I don't need magic or skills to do it.* Well, they don't let just anybody run the guild's help desk. She must have had her head screwed on straight, that's for sure.

"Let's just hurry up and see the paperwork, Miss Receptionist."

"Y-yes. I'll go fetch it now..." Looking a little flustered, she disappeared into the back.

"Master, you don't seem to be satisfied letting her off that lightly. Are you sure you didn't want to teach her a lesson?"

"No. Don't forget why we came here at the crack of dawn. It'll all be for nothing if we get into a fight with her."

"I suppose so, but I do detest the thought of being looked down upon by such an ignorant cow."

My dear Minnalis seemed even more irritable than usual today. Of course, I felt the same way she did toward the receptionist, but so long as she gave us what we wanted, I really couldn't care less.

"Here are the registration forms. For one copper, we can fill it out on your behalf. Do you need us to?"

"No, thanks."

I took the two sheets of paper, handed one to Minnalis, and started filling out the fields. When we had both finished our forms, I handed them back to the receptionist.

"Kaito and Minnalis, ages seventeen and sixteen. Races, human and Lagonid. And you both fight with swords, I see. Party name, 'Scorn Road.' Is this correct?"

"Yes, thank you."

"Then I'll make your guild cards now. It'll take a few moments, so please take a seat." The receptionist gestured to a sofa. Then she pointed to the bookshelf next to it. "The books there should fill you in on the finer workings of the guild. I can also give you a verbal overview later if you'd like, but since it seems you can read and write, please peruse them while I go and prepare your cards. There are also bestiaries detailing the trophy parts and weaknesses of various monsters, and field guides describing what kinds of medicinal and poisonous herbs you might come across. Feel free to read them at your leisure. I won't be long."

After saying all she was required to say, the receptionist left. Since I didn't feel like twiddling my thumbs, I picked a small text about how to be an adventurer from the shelves. Minnalis was also literate, so I picked out a book for her titled *Poisons and Medicines*. Her

"Intoxicating Phantasm" skill allowed her to create poisons, so perhaps it was worth it for her to learn a bit more about them.

As for me, I had already scanned pretty much every monster, poison, and medicine I'd come across with my Eight-Eyed Sword of Clarity, so I could access the data at any time. What interested me more right now was how the Adventurers Guild operated. The last time, they had elevated me to the top rank immediately once they realized I was a hero, so I didn't really have a clear handle on how the job actually worked.

...Or so I thought.

Unfortunately, the book didn't tell me anything I didn't already know.

"Increase your rank by doing jobs to increase the number of requests you can take on."

"Adventurers pay no fee to enter and leave cities."

"The guild's backing makes it easy to cross borders, even in times of war."

There were only a few small details that had escaped my knowledge until now. Apparently, there was a party rank in addition to our individual ranks. A party could be treated as, say, D rank if it could fight on par with a D-rank adventurer, even if was comprised of only E-rank adventurers. This would allow them to take on D-rank quests.

And there was one other point of interest; something that hadn't mattered to me when I was a hero last time. Entry into dungeons controlled by the countries or the guild was only permitted to adventurers of D rank and above.

That was quite inconvenient for us.

Of course, we were well equipped to handle a dungeon already, but I hadn't wanted to raise my status so soon for fear of attracting unwanted attention. Especially not now, before I had the chance to return to full strength and take care of anyone who came snooping my way.

I'd have to discuss this with Minnalis later, I thought.

Once I finished extracting what information I could from the title, I turned to the back cover, where there was a pyramid chart with seven rungs labeled "Guild Rank Overview."

Beside each rank was a colored plate and a brief description. From SSS, reading downward, they said:

SSS (White) : Legend, hero of folklore
SS (Black) : Inhuman levels of strength
                  (Only a few every 50 years)
S (Red) : Super genius (Only a few every decade)
A (Green) : Genius (Only a few every year)
B (Yellow) : Top-rate worker
C (Brown) : Veteran Adventurer
D (Blue) : Fully fledged
E (Gray) : Half-fledged
F (Purple) : Practically a beginner
Appr. (None) : Unable to register

There was no color listed for apprentices since they didn't receive a plate.

After looking it over, I returned the book to the shelf.

Come to think of it, nothing bad has happened yet. Was I overthinking things? I wondered.

Not a second later, I realized I had thought that too soon.

"Ha-ha-ha!! What luck! Never thought we'd come across an Oral Rabbit!"

"Yeah, they's sneaky bastards, that's for sure."

"Let's turn it in! I can't wait to see how much it's worth!"

Three adventurers suddenly walked in through the front door, needlessly belting out their plans to all within earshot. One was a woman with a mole beneath her left eye and curly dark hair that came down to her shoulders. The second, a short fellow with drooping eyes and spiky blond hair. And the third, an educated-looking gentleman with narrow eyes and black hair that was quite long for a man.

As they glanced over at me, a sensation like lightning crawled under my skin. That was something I didn't expect to feel today. It rose up in my throat, thick and burning, hope and pain mixed together. So bitter, and yet so, so sweet.

"...Ah... I guess I really am cursed."

Fate had no regard for me. It always came. No matter how much I hacked and hacked to sever it from my existence, I couldn't cut it away from me. Oh well. If this was destiny, then so be it. I didn't know if this was good luck or bad, and to be honest, it didn't make one blind bit of difference. Curse or no, there was only one thing that mattered.

Standing right there were the people I longed to kill.

Ahhh, who would've thought they'd show up here!

The woman with the mole, the leader, she was called Zuily. The short, blond-haired scout was Dot, and the black-haired man with the bow on his back was Terry. And there was one missing. One more person who ought to have been with them. The cheeky mage kid who always bragged about how he used to be a noble: Hansel.

Dammit, I don't have enough info on them yet.

My shallow relationship with them meant I didn't have a lot of data to go on. I had originally met them somewhere else, and all I knew about them was their names, how strong they were, and their general personalities.

Ahhh, how frustrating.

I picked up a bestiary and pretended to flip through the pages as I watched them carefully. Sure enough, eventually, one other person entered the guild. A short boy with bright blond hair, wearing leather armor beneath his brown robe, and carrying a staff in one hand.

"...Ahhh, *there* you are."

I covered my face with my hand to conceal the grin that rose to my lips unbidden. Through my fingers, I watched as Hansel peered around the guild and approached the reception desk. My blood raced, burning my body as if molten rocks had been dropped into my veins.

I'm sure the right thing to do would be to forgive what these people had done. If they kept to themselves, there'd be no reason to kill them. Perhaps I would have agreed, long before the scales of my heart were tipped.

After all, it wasn't so clear-cut whether or not these guys had betrayed me. I won't try to pretend that my blood and flesh were immediately wreathed in flame, transforming into bubbling poison the instant I saw them.

But... Ahhh, it was no use. I couldn't forgive them. Not a single bit of me wanted to.

I'll seal them underground and wrap them in cold flames. I'll use red-hot iron bars to suck all the moisture from their bodies. I'll burn them blacker and blacker until nothing remains but ash. I'll kill the bastards. Kill them all.

...The scales of my heart tipped to one side with nary a quiver of hesitation.

CHAPTER 2
Memories of Solace Aflame and the Pit of Melting Flesh

It was a dream, sickeningly sweet and so, so distant.

But it wasn't just a dream. It was also a memory. A memory of a demon lord and of her hero.

☆

I could hear the sounds of calling birds. The sun's light rained down on me, as if trying to make me forget this violent world, instead blanketing me in its warmth.

"Hey. Shouldn't our places be swapped?" I asked.

A sudden breeze filled my nostrils with the soft aroma of flowers and sent lightly colored petals scattering through the air. Somewhere mixed in alongside them was the sweet smell of her hair.

We were in a beautiful field beside an abandoned church hidden deep within the forest. Verdant ivy bursting with life scaled the crumbling walls, shocking in their vigor. I was resting beneath a single tree, my legs extended before me, with Leticia's head on my lap.

"Hmm? What? I won today, so you have to be nice to me. That means you have to do everything I say!"

Her voice was like the soothing sound of a small bell.

"But aren't I also nice to you when I win? Oh well, fine by me either way."

"I don't recall asking you to stop stroking! Gently! Put some love into it, for crying out loud!"

"Yeah, yeah."

"Mhm! Hm-hm-hm!"

As I pretended to be fed up, I gently stroked her soft, silky hair. She didn't need to tell me to be gentle. It all came naturally. With a smile on her face, she nuzzled her head against my lap.

"Coochie-coo!"

"Hey, cut that out! It tickles! What are you doing?"

"Hee-hee... Just wanted to see how you'd react. Think nothing of it. Coochie-coo!"

Oh god. She'd turned into an idiot.

And yet I couldn't find it within myself to be annoyed. I could only think of how cute she was. How precious she was to me.

"I'll get you back for that!" I warned.

"Hey! Wh-whoooah! K-Kaito! Didn't I say you have to be nice to me? I'll not stand for this insubordination!"

I squeezed her in my arms, giving her a noogie. She kicked and flailed, but she seemed to enjoy it.

"Hnyah!"

"Oh?"

The noise she made was so cute, I wondered if I might have been too rough. Wriggling herself free and sitting up straight, Leticia started pounding on me with her fists.

"You're messing up my hair!" she cried.

"Ha-ha, sorry. Come on, lie back down."

"Hmmrh... Okay, but you'd better be gentle this time."

"Gotcha. I'll be as gentle as a mouse."

She lay down once more, and I began straightening out her disheveled hair. I didn't want to let the feeling of a single strand slip through my fingers, even if it meant I had to heighten my senses to combat level. Even I realized how oddly I was acting. It was totally uncharacteristic of me, and I knew I'd only look back in shame afterward. When did I become like this?

"Mmm... Whaa... Kaitooo..."

But all those thoughts faded away when Leticia called my name.

"Leticia."

"Mm... Mmrh? Wh-what are you doing?!"

Before I could stop myself, I had kissed her hair. Once she realized what I had just done, her face flushed, and she became giddy with happiness.

...Why the heck is she so darn cute?

"It's not fair! You're too adorable!" I claimed.

"Hey, no! Uuu!"

I could hold myself back no longer, and I hugged her with all my might.

We were happy. I wanted to stay like this forever. For the first time ever since coming to this world, I wanted this moment to last.

"Kaito, you oaf! You complete and utter fool!"

"Yeah, I'm a fool, all right. You're the one who said I should be nice to you."

I couldn't believe how content I was. I never thought being in love would make me this way.

"Mrh... That's *too* nice," said Leticia. "If you keep this up, you might forget how to hold back when we're in public."

"Hmm... That would be bad."

"Yes, it would! I can't have you acting like this when I go to your world and meet your parents! It would be too embarrassing!"

"Yeah, and Mai would say something like 'You animal, Kaito!' …
Oh god, I don't think I would ever live it down…"

I could just see my sister fuming at me.

Actually, it's been two years since then. Perhaps she's changed.
I have no idea what happened after I left. I guess they most likely
assumed I'd run away from home. I really wish I could say sorry to
them. To Mom and Dad, and to Mai, too.

"…Someone loves his sister a little too much!"

"Ha-ha, jealous?"

"Yes!"

We glared into each other's eyes. Then after a short while, neither
of us could stand it any longer, and we fell about laughing.

I wanted to go back home; I always did. But today, for once, I felt
glad I was summoned here.

And anyway, it would still be some time before I could figure out
how to take her with me.

I was a different man now. I had grown strong as a hero.

So it doesn't matter. In this world or in mine. We'll always be…

"Leticia…"

"Mm…"

I found myself drawn toward her and planted my lips on hers.

"Raorl!"

""Wh-wha?! Ah!""

A sudden bark made us fly apart in shock. A single garm was
looking at us. It was about puppy-size—though if it were fully
grown it would be much larger than a dog—and it had a distinctive
crescent-shaped white marking on the fur of its neck.

"Hey, why do you do this every time…?"

"G-grrrrr…"

Leticia and I both wore the same flabbergasted, red-faced

expression, though it was hard to say whether it was embarrassment at being seen or anger at being interrupted.

"Hawoo?" The garm pup gave a confused howl and, as usual, I found myself unable to say any more.

"Jesus Christ. Here, this is what you're after, isn't it?"

"Rawr! ♪"

I took some monster meat from my sack and tossed it over. The garm pup began chewing at it happily.

"I don't know when you got so used to shaking us down all the time."

This was all because I decided on a whim to give it some of our spare food that one time. It was just so shaky. It looked starved. Now, every time we're here, it comes back for more.

"There, there. Hungry boy. Make sure you eat it all and grow up big and strong," cooed Leticia, petting the garm on the head.

"I thought you were supposed to be sulking."

"What's this? Jealous much?"

"Yeah, so take care of me, too."

"My, what a hopeless fool you are. Mn."

We kissed again.

Those days were like a dream. Those days where all we did was repeat tired old phrases to each other. They were the best days of my life.

"...Ghah... Hah..."

Shoot. I only meant to rest a while beneath this tree, but I fell asleep. The remains of my sweet escape from reality drifted around me, making the world before me taste all the more bitter in comparison.

How did it all end up like this? I hugged my own injured body tightly and pressed on into the dark woods.

After my fight with Leticia, I had returned only to be ambushed by my allies. I barely escaped with my life. And it wasn't just my friends who were after me. All the soldiers and adventurers I had brought with me for the final battle had turned on me as well. Some mad demon of war must have taken control of them all, exploiting our exhaustion in the conflict's aftermath. It was the only explanation.

"Grr... Dammit!"

With the wounds on my heart and my skin still fresh, I advanced unsteadily into the black depths of the forest. Eventually I came upon the ruined remains of that church, and the field where I went with Leticia all that time ago.

"Ha-ha... I said I would rescue her, but I killed her, with my own hands. I'm such an irredeemable bastard."

I never wanted to fight her. I knew there was no other way. But knowing that and accepting it were two different things.

And so I lingered in the scent of days gone by. Even though I knew there was no going back. Even though I still had a promise to fulfill.

Oh, how wretched and pitiable I must have seemed.

Suddenly, I sensed an approaching monster.

"Heh. How did it get so close before I noticed? I must really be losing it."

I turned to spot a small garm standing in the bushes.

"That neck marking... You're the one from back then..."

"Ruff!"

Some time had passed, and the pup had grown up. Now it was even larger than a regular garm.

"...Your leg's hurt. Guess the guys chasing me must have gotten hold of you."

The wound had clearly been made by a blade. This was no turf war with another monster.

"Let's find shelter, and I'll patch you up."

The garm looked in pain, so I scooped it up and took it inside the ruined church. It wasn't exactly pleasant, but it was better than staying out in the freezing rain.

"Sorry about this. Usually, it wouldn't take me so long to heal one wound…"

I had lost my pack during the battle, and with it, all my expensive items. All I had left now were basic potions.

"Haoo…"

I grabbed one at random, poured it onto the wounds, and made some bandages by cutting up my underclothes with a knife. Monsters were tough. It wouldn't succumb to an injury like this.

"Ha-ha, you're all beat up. Just like me…"

"Gwar."

I softly stroked the garm's head, and it offered no resistance.

"Now, you rest here for the night. I'll bet that wound will be gone by morning."

Once I left the forest, my friends would follow me and leave this place alone. The pup seemed quite tired, and as I gently stroked its head, it soon began to breathe softly.

"…"

I wanted nothing more than to lay my head down and rest, too, but one of the soul blades I had used in the battle made it so I couldn't sleep for another two days.

I would leave this place for now. Perhaps one day, I could return and sit down once more beneath that tree where Leticia and I had kissed.

The moon peeked through the clouds. The rain had stopped, and I was bathed in moonlight.

Though I was still terribly injured, I felt like the memory of those days had eased my pain a little, but the smell of the flowers and the colors of their petals were the same as they ever were, and a single tear rolled down my cheek.

"Flame Multilance!"

"Wh-what?!"

In a second, *it all went up in flames.* A hail of fiery spears flew in and laid waste to that peaceful place. The inferno engulfed the field, licking at the beautiful flowers like the tongues of a million red snakes. All I could hear was a crackle. All I could smell was the scent of burning plants, and all I could see was a world of crimson and orange death.

"What are you doing?! I told you to kill him in one hit!!"

"We're up against that monster; I'm taking no chances!"

An army of adventurers stepped out of the forest. There were four of them at the head of the group.

Their names were Zuily, Dot, Terry, and Hansel.

"Well, we have little choice now. Surround him and kill him!" shouted the leader, Zuily.

"Where do you think you're going? You may seem like a monster, but you're a human just like us! If we just keep pounding you with spells, you'll die soon enough!"

"Kh?!"

Normally I could shrug off magic like this even if I was buck naked, but the fight with Leticia had worn me down, and bit by bit, their incantations were damaging me.

Their fire magic was just as I had taught them. Total coverage, leaving no escape.

It wouldn't be hard for me to fight back, but I might end up killing them, or at the very least, leave them with wounds from which they'd never recover.

Once more, a wave of flames washed across the field.

"Stop! Come back to your senses!"

This was the place was where I'd made so many memories!

It was the symbol of my happiness!

"Don't burn it… Please… Leave this place alone!"

But my words, too, were engulfed by the blaze.

"Hey, no slacking. Keep the fires going."

"I get it, I get it, Zuily. I *am* a former noble, you know. I've no objections to defeating an evil hero who's turned against humanity. Spears of flame, heed my call. *Fire Lance!*"

With a roar, the magic spears flew across the land, reducing all those beautiful flowers to ash.

Fire. It was everywhere. It was all burning.

The one thing Leticia left for me. The only treasure I had remaining. It was being taken from me.

Why? Why was this happening?

"Ghr! Stop! Stop it!!" I begged and pleaded too many times to count.

"Dot, Terry, don't let up on the oil! If we can take down the evil hero, we'll be famous!"

"Roger, boss!"

"Hmph. Leave it to me."

The helpless flowers were trampled underfoot. Just like my memories of that day.

"You lot, too! We'll be rich if we can pull this job off! Put your backs into it!"

""""Yeah!!""""

At Zuily's order, the magical artillery ramped up their assault.

One stray fireball descended upon the ruined church.

"No… No!!"

That's where the garm pup is sleeping…!!

I leaped into the air to shield the building from the reckless spell. If it collapsed, the garm would have no time to escape before it was crushed to death.

But my action only made things worse.

"Now! *Flame Bullet!*"

Spotting his chance, Hansel took aim and unleashed a fast-moving spell. However, in his haste, he neglected to aim properly, and the fireball rushed toward the church.

I was still off-balance from blocking the first. There was no way I could stop a second.

I could do nothing but watch as the projectile flew uninterrupted into the stone building, blasting it to rubble.

"Ahhh... Aahhh... Aaaahhh..."

The fiery fragments fell to earth before my eyes, and what remained of the ruined church crumbled to the ground.

That was all I was looking at.

It hurts. It hurts. My heart screamed, and strength left me.

I couldn't even raise my arms to protect my face as hundreds of spells tore into me from all angles. The inferno razed that place to the ground along with my happy memories.

The flowers we laughed among were burning.

The tree we sat against as we played with the garm was ablaze.

And now, before my eyes, that garm was crushed beneath the church, our special place.

"Looking good. Now let's finish him o—"

"RrraaaaaaaaaaaAAAAAAAAAARRRGGHH!!"

*   *   *

Before I could even register what I was doing, I had flattened everyone who stood near me.

"Hrrh…hrrh…hrrh…hrrh…"

Soon nothing remained but the scorched earth, littered with fallen adventurers, and the smoldering rubble that was once a church.

"Haah…gh…haah…haah…"

I dragged my body over to the pile of stones and frantically began pulling them aside. I knew what I was going to find, but I didn't stop digging. I couldn't.

"Haah…aahhh…aaagh…gh…grh…rgh… I'm sorry… I'm so sorry…"

And just as I knew I would, I dug up the poor thing's *remains*.

I cradled its body in my arms. It was cold, so cold that the hot tears falling down my cheeks felt like lies.

"…Argh. Goddammit, you bastards… I knew it…"

That's right. That was, this is, a dream of the past. My mind was replaying over and over all the pain I'd suffered. Taunting me with this nightmare that was reality.

"Dammit… I get it… I get it already…"

That's right. This was my truth. Not a dream. My memories of those days. Just as those happy days were like sweet nectar to me, so too was I constantly reminded of life's bitter taste, like needles in my mouth.

"Life is a cruel joke. That's all it's ever been…"

A little later, I found out my friends weren't being controlled after all.

What's done is done. You can't undo it any more than you can unbreak an egg or unspill water.

Even if the world was rewound, things could never go back to the way they were.

Even if this were a dream. No, because it was a dream.

"Argh, dammit. I really needed that."

All I could do was cry. It felt like life was telling me that none of it was real. That my shining treasure had no more value than burning garbage.

So yeah. I'm gonna have to kill you after all.

I can't allow you to get away with this.

Even if I wanted to, I couldn't. But I don't.

Perhaps you were deceived. Perhaps you were only doing your job.

Perhaps you didn't know what you were doing when you attacked me. But you know...

That place did nothing to you. And you didn't care how much it meant to me. You didn't care about the life you snuffed out that night.

To you, it was just a church. An old ruin. Just a field of flowers with a single old tree. And the beast you killed, nothing more than a monster.

But to me, it was one of the few precious things Leticia had left me.

To me, it was a life that could never be replaced.

A memory of bygone days and the existence of a single monster. ..."I didn't know" just isn't going to cut it.

"Master, it's unwise to fall asleep here."

"Mmh…mmrh…"

A sweet voice gently roused me from my slumber, and a soft hand rocked me awake.

"Hwah… Minnalis… Sorry, guess I dozed off."

I shook my head, and bit by bit, my mind began to clear. We had split up to do the shopping, and I had arrived at our meetup spot a little early. I had sat down on a bench in the town square to stare at the clouds while I waited for Minnalis to arrive, and I suppose the warm rays of the sun must have put me to sleep.

"How did it go? Did you find the things we need?"

"Yes, and I managed to get them quite cheaply, too!" Minnalis smiled.

"Oh, nice."

Then, as if on cue, both of our stomachs growled. Going by the position of the sun, it was probably about time for lunch, anyway. We had gotten up early, so we were famished by now.

"Let's get some food while we have the chance."

"Indeed, I'm quite peckish."

I stood up from the bench and started walking.

No matter how calm I appeared, I couldn't get that lot out of my head. All I could think about was what I had seen a few hours prior at the guild.

"Minnalis, I've decided to end their lives."

She heard the clank of my scales falling cleanly to one side.

"…Understood, Master."

She grasped what I was feeling immediately and gave a single nod.

Minnalis shared in my revenge. While the overlap of our mem-ories wasn't perfect and there were many gaps, this part, at least, seemed to work as intended.

Now, what to do next? I replayed the facts in my head.

When Hansel had arrived at the guild, he hadn't called out to his teammates. Instead, he had gone right up to the counter next to ours, speaking to a receptionist a little older than the one we had spoken with, perhaps to the point she could be called a veteran.

"I'm here to be an adventurer. Proceed with the formalities."

Using my mana to enhance my hearing, I could pick out Han-sel's arrogant voice.

He's here to register...? So he isn't with Zuily's party yet.

I clicked my tongue silently. It would be hard to keep track of them all if they weren't together. Not the biggest problem in the world, but it sure made things difficult.

"You're here to be an adventurer? Understood."

"If you have time to repeat my own words back to me, then snap to it, woman!"

The receptionist shrugged off Hansel's words and politely con-tinued the conversation, but at each stage, she was hounded by tales of his house's former glory and unreasonable requests. I didn't envy her position.

"I think we can leave him be for now, Master."

"Yeah. What about Zuily and the others?"

While Hansel and the receptionist were locked in pointless strug-gle, I turned my attention over to the other group. The three of them were eating breakfast together in the tavern at the guild. They had each ordered some rather expensive items and appeared to be enjoy-ing a celebratory meal. Clearly, they had been partying all night prior to this, too, for their faces were still flushed red with alcohol. It seemed they had been returning from an orc-slaying quest when they happened upon the Oral Rabbit and, with great difficulty, took the thing down.

An Oral Rabbit was a rabbitlike monster about a half meter in length, with small horns and a mouth that looked like it had been torn open. Its attack and defense were zero, but it had a ridiculously high speed and an ability that allowed it to camouflage into its surroundings. All this made it a surprisingly tough opponent. Above all, they were rare. With their heightened senses, they could disappear before a predator got close, making them incredibly hard to find. It was for these reasons that, despite their utter lack of combat ability, they were D-rank creatures. However, their meat was a delicacy, their organs had medicinal properties, and the horns and claws could be used to make powerful magic items. Even their fur was prized for its softness and warmth. Therefore, the reward for catching one was high. Just a single specimen could net you enough money to live off for a whole month.

So that's why they're here so early in the morning.

They seemed to have captured the Oral Rabbit late at night, and by the time they'd returned to town, it was still before dawn. Obviously, the guild was closed, and so instead of returning to their lodgings, they had frequented some of their favorite pubs while they waited for the guild to open for the day.

"…" I watched them laugh and make merry, just as they had done when they'd burned my field of flowers to the ground.

"Right, then. I'd say it's about time we turn this thing in."

Zuily rose from her seat and, still a little giddy, made her way over to the reception desk.

"…Hmm? What's this…?"

Just then, something happened I wasn't expecting. Zuily headed to the very same desk Hansel was using.

"Outta the way, kid. Can't ya see I got shit to do?"

"H-how dare you! Are you drunk?"

"Ah-ha-ha, looks like things are about to get interesting."

"It appears to be turning into a quarrel, Master."

Zuily was drunkenly picking a fight, while Hansel seemed quite taken aback by a member of his dream profession acting so unseemly, adding fuel to the fire with remarks like "Aren't you ashamed to be hammered so early in the morning?" and "This is why you'll never go up a rank!"

Obviously, Zuily wasn't one to take this kind of slander lying down, all the more so because it had spoiled her good mood. While content to taunt him at first, she gradually grew more and more heated, spilling out clichés such as "What does a brat like you know?" or "Adventuring isn't all sunshine and rainbows."

Under the watchful eye of the guild, their spat was unlikely to become more than a conflict of words; otherwise, they might have lunged at each other's throats already. Scuffles like this, though, happened every day, and the guild wouldn't bother intervening in every little argument that transpired on its doorstep.

Which meant there seemed to be no end in sight for these two.

Now, I wonder what will happen next...?

The timing couldn't have been more perfect. I had been wanting to find out more about these four so I could think of ways to kill them. All I had to do now was sit back and watch, without drawing any attention to myself...

"Kaito, Minnalis! Your cards are ready!"

"Read the room, newbie...!!"

The receptionist had been in such a hurry to get back to me she hadn't even noticed the argument going on right before her eyes.

"Shall I turn her into mincemeat, Master?" asked Minnalis.

I had looked right at her when she called my name. There was no pretending I hadn't heard her now.

"...No need. In fact, this might work out in our favor."

I had wanted to watch the fight a little longer, but what was done was done. It wouldn't even be too bad if I were to get involved. That way, I could guide the flow to my advantage.

In any case, getting our identification came first.

"There are your guild cards. We charge five silver pieces for replacements, so please try not to lose them."

The receptionist handed us two pale yellow slips about the size of a credit card. They felt like plastic, but supposedly they were made of some special monster material.

"Please let out a little blood onto the cards. That will register them with you."

The receptionist handed over a pair of needles with which I pricked the tip of my finger. As the blood dribbled onto the card, it shone momentarily with a pale glow, before returning to normal.

"The registration process is complete. The information on the card can only be read by the owner, or by the guild through the use of one of our magic items."

With the card in my hand, I focused, and sure enough, words appeared on the surface.

STATUS

Name: Kaito

Age: 17

Race: Human

Fighting Style: Swordsman

Adventurer Rank: F

Party Rank: F

Party Name: Scorn Road

Name: Minnalis

Age: 16

Race: Lagonid

Fighting Style: Swordswoman

Adventurer Rank: F

Party Rank: F

Party Name: Scorn Road

Minnalis did the same, and similar information appeared on hers.

"Also, here is the plate signifying your adventurer rank. Since you are currently F rank, the plate is purple. If you show this at a checkpoint, any entry fees will be waived, so don't forget to take it with you whenever you leave the city on your quests."

"Do we need to wear it somewhere visible?"

"No, you simply have to present it when entering and exiting. Since it acts as a status symbol of sorts for experienced adventurers, some people prefer to wear it at all times."

I could see the sense in that. Speaking as a mild-mannered earthling, I knew there wasn't a single place in this world you couldn't expect to get into some sort of brawl. Wearing something to show you could handle yourself was a smart idea. At the very least, it would keep all but the most foolhardy from trying to pick a fight with you.

All the while, the pointless argument beside me was still going. At some point, Zuily's two friends had come over to back her up. Hansel, finding himself outnumbered three-to-one, was looking in our direction, as if asking for help.

We were about his age and newbie adventurers just like him. Maybe he thought he could buddy up with us. In fact, he definitely thought that.

So when we turned to leave without a single word, he called out to us.

"Hey! You guys agree with me, right?"

"Huh? Uh... About what?"

Inwardly, I was smirking my largest smirk. As always, his stupidity had saved us. Now it wouldn't be the least bit suspicious if I were to get involved.

"That it's cheap hacks like these who are bringing down the reputation of the adventuring profession, getting drunk in the wee hours of the morning just because they happened upon a rare monster that's not even very strong!"

"Huh?! You think I'm gonna let you get away with that, punk?"

"C'mon, Zuily, just let it go…"

Dot moved to restrain his partner, and Terry pointed with his eyes to one of the reception desks. There, a gruff old man watched the fight closely, his eyes half open as he sat in his chair. His muscles weren't just for show. It was usually retired veterans who took this job.

"Okay, well, I heard a bit of what you were saying earlier. How about this? We were just about to head out on a monster-slaying quest. Why don't we settle it by seeing who can hunt the most beasts?" I suggested.

That seemed to get their attention.

"You're never going to settle anything by shouting at each other, so instead of going outside and beating each other up, why not have a true test of an adventurer's mettle? Whoever wins gets the reward money from all of them. There's no problem with that, is there?"

I addressed this last part to the receptionist, who answered, "N-no. Private exchange of cash between adventurers is not allowed, but this sort of thing would not technically be against the rules."

Private exchange of cash between adventurers was not allowed. This was a rule put in place to prevent innocent young novices from getting ripped off in precisely this kind of scenario. It wasn't a crime, but the guild imposed heavy sanctions.

In other words, if they tried to settle things themselves, neither of them would come out on top. It would only sate their own egos.

"*Tsk.* Well, whatever, we could do with a distraction."

Zuily glanced over at Hansel before replying. She seemed to have sobered up a little. Even without her partners, there was no way she would lose to this pip-squeak. As she eyed the young mage, it was clear she grasped just how much stronger she was than him.

Still, magic was a powerful art, and even a glancing blow could sometimes be fatal. She would have to be stupid to want to get into a physical altercation with him.

"I have no objections, myself," replied the boy. "In fact, I welcome the challenge. What shall be our game?"

"Ha, as if F-rank losers get the luxury of choice," spat Zuily as she tore a flyer off the request board. "Here, this is all they've got for the likes of you."

It was a request to slay goblins. Fifty-four of them, with an additional bonus paid for each one after that.

"You want more, you're gonna have to raise your rank a bit, ain't ya?" she said, waving the flyer in his direction.

"*Harrumph.* I may only be F rank, but I warn you: I'm a talented mage. I've mastered the Fire Lance spell. In terms of raw talent, I'm ten times the adventurer you'll ever be!!"

Zuily's eyes narrowed a little in suspicion. Fire Lance was quite a difficult incantation to master. It had high power and an MP consumption rate to match, and it was almost impossible to control. Being able to cast it would give him more than enough reason to strut around like he was God's gift to wizardkind.

...Well, if he could cast it by himself, that is.

I shifted my gaze to the staff in his hand, and I identified it as providing "Fire Magic Support." It was a good-quality item, too. Its price was probably measured in gold coins.

Apparently Zuily noticed it, too, for her eyes suddenly became filled with greed as deep as a swamp.

I touched the Eight-Eyed Sword of Clarity hanging at my waist and looked at Zuily's status screen.

"...My, my, what's this?"

"I see, Master. That explains it."

Minnalis and I softly conferred while the others were distracted with their own conversation. My partner in crime could see what I could see. And there, in the field for intrinsic abilities, there were the words...

... *"Nose for Gold"*

"Well, this should make things interesting."

"Indeed. So it shall."

I looked once more at the four, who had somehow started another argument.

Zuily. Dot. Terry. Hansel.

I don't know how you four became associates and came to stand before me that day. I don't know, but it no longer matters. And I know it wasn't only you there, and you were just the leaders of a larger band, but that no longer matters, either.

You weren't the first people to attack me, and you were far from the last. I don't remember every single time I got into a scrape, and I didn't have the luxury of learning the names of every last delinquent who came after me.

So I suppose you all are simply unlucky.

Out of all the people in the crowd that day, you were the four I happened to remember.

Out of all the people in town this morning, you were the four I happened to run into.

Out of all the people in this world, you four happened to cross me.

I know your pain. After all...

Out of all 7.3 billion people on Earth, I happened to be the one summoned to this world.

So I'm afraid that's all there is to it.

*   *   *

Tough luck.

"Ahhh, I can't wait." I chuckled, taking no pains to conceal my voice.

This time, the second time, the story you four would go on to weave shall be cut tragically short.

"I can't wait."

The only thoughts in my head were about how I was going to make them suffer.

In the end, we agreed upon a nearby forest as the location for the hunt, which would begin the next day, with the winner being whoever could hunt the most goblins by sunset. The one flaw in my brilliant plan was that while I had intended to remain a neutral mediator for this debate, I seemed to have ended up dragged onto Hansel's side. It was all because he had complained that three against one would be unfair. His opponents, too, agreed they didn't want to develop a reputation as the team that had to gang up to defeat a helpless newbie. And so, whether I liked it or not, I would be joining the fray.

I had tried suggesting they settle it one-on-one instead, but Hansel had insisted that the other two might still try to help her out. Perhaps I could have continued to argue the point, but by that time, the place was getting a little lively. I didn't want to attract any more attention than I already had, so I left it at that.

I also didn't want to make it seem like I had any grudge with the other team. To that end, I stipulated that Minnalis and I be left out of the wager, though our kills would still count toward victory. In other words, should Zuily's team win, they would only get the reward money for the goblins Hansel killed. Conversely, should our team win, Hansel would get the other party's entire bounty to himself. That way, Minnalis and I technically had no stake in the outcome. Dot and Terry were a little hesitant that this unfairly favored the boy, but they shut their mouths when I pointed out we were the ones getting wrapped up in their mess. After all, we were a couple of newbie adventurers who supposedly had never even met before today. Our opponents, meanwhile, were an experienced party who had been working together for many years.

In return, we agreed Hansel should pay up for all three of us, regardless of how much work he actually did. That way, if Zuily's team won, we wouldn't be able to cheat them out of their money by claiming it was all Minnalis and me.

While all this was going on, Zuily herself was not really contributing to the conversation, her eyes flitting instead to Hansel's staff and Minnalis.

They were the muddy eyes of greed, no doubt. She was not a hard woman to read. She was probably thinking about what sort of price Minnalis would fetch as a slave. I usually didn't like when people subjected Minnalis to their degrading gaze, but Zuily's greed was so pure and obvious I almost couldn't help laughing.

After that, we had parted ways and arranged to meet up at the guild the next day. Zuily's party simply turned in the Oral Rabbit and left. They seemed not to have the slightest interest in what we got up to in the meantime, saying they were probably going to go get drunk someplace else.

"Well, we should probably get going, too," I announced. "We've got a lot to mull over before tomorrow."

"Yes, Master."

"Ah, hold on, could I speak to you for one second?"

Just as we were about to leave, Hansel stopped us. To be honest, I just wanted to get out of there as soon as possible. The contest was tomorrow, and for the moment, my involvement was still an *accident*. I couldn't allow this opportunity to pass me by. There was precious little time, and I still had a lot of thinking to do if I was going to come up with the best way of killing them.

"I wanted to apologize for getting you two mixed up in all that. But I knew I could count on you. After all, we're the same, you and I. I was hoping we might talk things over before tomorrow, perhaps over breakfast? My treat."

It was difficult to hide the emotions welling up inside me. He disgusted me. He was getting on my nerves, even though it was clear he didn't mean it. I sensed no ill will from him, and yet I wondered if he was hiding something. What did he mean, we're the same?

Then I realized. He probably thought I was a noble just like him. *Then he feels like he has an affinity with us. Or rather, with me.*

It wasn't as if it were rare for adventurers to own slaves, but for a greenhorn like myself? There weren't many other possibilities. Besides an adventurer, who else but a noble was rich enough to buy slaves? The son of a wealthy merchant, perhaps, but that was about it.

I smiled and shrugged my shoulders. "Sorry, we've already eaten. And don't worry about it. People like us should stick together."

There was a limit to how well I could keep up appearances, and I was already falling apart.

"I see. Well, in that case, should we emerge victorious tomorrow, supper shall be on me," he offered, before returning to the reception desk to finish his registration. We watched him speak to the receptionist lady, then turned and left the building.

After leaving, I took a deep sigh to cool myself off. Then I brought up a subject totally unrelated to the matter of torturing and killing at hand.

"I never realized people would assume I was a noble just because I'm a beginner adventurer with a slave, but I suppose it makes sense," I theorized.

I had intentionally not taken pains to hide Minnalis's Slave Brand, hoping to mitigate the inevitable wave of suitors who would otherwise approach her. It appeared there was a side effect in doing so that I had not completely anticipated.

"Shall we obscure it, Master? I think most people have already seen it by now, though..."

"No, I don't think we have to do that. It's not the most inconvenient thing in the world if people think I'm a noble. In fact, it'd be more annoying if we tried to hide it and people found out."

I pondered the issue for a while, and then continued.

"If people think you're not a slave, we'll have to deal with the riff-raff flocking to you. Adventurers in particular. They won't care about how you're a beastfolk or a demihuman or whatnot. And with how pretty you are, they'll come in droves."

"...There you go, exaggerating again, Master. I'm not that pretty."

Minnalis remained expressionless, apparently unconvinced. Perhaps she was blushing on the inside? It was hard to tell if she was using that skill of hers or not. On the off chance she really didn't realize how beautiful she was and the effect she could have on others, I decided to make it clear.

"No, you are that gorgeous, without a doubt. As far as I'm concerned, you're the sweetest thing on this Earth. Ask any man off the street and they'll agree."

"...Huh."

Even that didn't seem to induce the slightest bit of emotion.

Though I had only meant it as a simple statement of fact, I still felt a little flustered at having said that out loud and quickly got back to the point.

"I'm just saying I don't want to have to deal with every random guy who figures they might have a chance with you. I'm not going to go around killing them all, either. Besides..."

"…Yes?"

"Any piece of shit who tries to steal you away knowing you're my slave will make for a fine guinea pig to test our torture methods on. After all, those goblins couldn't talk back, so how could we know how effective it was?"

I had decided not to get any innocent bystanders involved in my vengeance. I had many reasons, but mainly I didn't think my heart could take it. And I didn't think I could ever face Leticia again if I did. It would be like throwing everything she had given me into the trash.

So I avoided killing people unrelated to my revenge.

…But that presupposes that they were, in fact, a person.

Someone who disregards all dignity and acts only on base impulses isn't worthy of being considered a person. They're a monster.

Someone to not only be slaughtered but made into useful materials.

"…Haah, so we ended up going there after all."

My train of thought somehow returned to the issue of getting the most effective and satisfying vengeance. Was it all I could think about?

Well, that's okay. Even if it is…that's all I am now. A being of revenge.

"All right."

After stocking up on medicines and poisons, we grabbed some lunch in town and headed back to the inn. Once in our room, we placed them all inside our bag and began our discussion in preparation for the next day. Taking the Eight-Eyed Sword of Clarity from my hip, I channeled a little mana into it to review all the data I'd collected in my travels.

There I found the status screens of Zuily and her party.

STATUS

Zuily   Lv43

Age 31 • Female • Human

HP: 682/682   MP: 569/569

Strength: 399   Stamina: 357

Vitality: 390   Agility: 418

Magic: 331   Resistance: 391

Intrinsic Abilities: Nose for Gold
Skills: Sword Lv 6, Track Lv 2, Stealth Lv 3,
Darkvision Lv 2, Acrobatics Lv 3,
Carve Lv 5, Fortification Magic Lv 3
Status: OK (Tipsy)

Dot

Lv37

Age 28 • Male • Human

HP: 561/561   MP: 348/348

Strength: 253   Stamina: 394

Vitality: 325   Agility: 457

Magic: 217   Resistance: 317

Intrinsic Abilities: None
Skills: Dagger Lv 4, Sword Lv 1, Track Lv 5,
Stealth Lv 3, Darkvision Lv 3, Acrobatics Lv 2
Notice Lv 2, Carve Lv 6,
Enhance Sight (S) Lv 2, Recon Lv 2
Status: OK (Tipsy)

Terry
Lv39

Age 29 • Male • Human

HP: 415/415   MP: 630/630

Strength: 94   Stamina: 214

Vitality: 275   Agility: 247

Magic: 549   Resistance: 499

Intrinsic Abilities: None
Skills: Bow Lv 3, Track Lv 1, Darkvision Lv 2,
Wind Magic Lv 2, Control Magic Lv 3,
Meditate Lv 3, Hawkeye Lv 2,
Carve Lv 5
Status: OK (Tipsy)

"The all-around sword-wielder in the lead, the speedy rogue for scouting, and the ranged bowman bringing up the rear, is it?" asked Minnalis.

"Add a powerful mage for some extra firepower, and their party's decently balanced."

When I first met them, Zuily was rank B+, and her associates were rank B, assuming they were telling the truth. That was three years in the future now, though. I didn't know for sure what rank they'd be now, but judging by their stats, I'd say they were at least two below that.

"Now, I can more or less guess from the name, but... Hmm..."

I turned my appraisal abilities on Zuily's intrinsic ability, Nose for Gold. Apparently it gave her an intuitive understanding of when she was looking at something expensive. The catch here was what exactly it considered pricey. It couldn't detect an item's abilities, like my Appraise could. Nor could it sense the magic power residing in an item, or even convey anything about its abilities to her at all. That was why it had reacted to Hansel's staff, but not to the Eight-Eyed Sword at my hip or any of my other soul blades, even though by any metric, they were far stronger. Nobody could use those weapons except me, and if someone tried to take them, they would vanish. Therefore, in terms of money, they were worthless.

"Now, how should we do it?" I closed the status screens.

"I have a few methods I haven't been able to test on monsters yet...," started Minnalis.

"No. Those are useful if we're trying to think up new ways to make people suffer, but by themselves, they're mainly for inflicting pain."

Since we couldn't talk to monsters, it was sometimes necessary to turn to harsher methods to get them to comply. A sharp dosage of pain was usually enough to trigger their survival instincts and allow us to experiment on them. But that was all Minnalis's methods could accomplish. Even if we could force our victims to perform complex tasks, it wasn't great for our purposes because there was no intention behind it, just instinct.

"Simply inflicting pain isn't the goal here. We want them to be bathed in fear, crying out in madness. Otherwise, it'll never be enough. So here's what we'll do. First, we'll............ Then we'll............, and then finally, we'll kill them."

I described to Minnalis one of the many torture methods floating around in my head.

"I see. I certainly agree that would be fun to watch. But is such a thing even possible?"

"Maybe? We can try it on a goblin first. Let's grab lunch and head out."

I stood up from the table, and she followed suit.

"But that doesn't seem like it would be very painful. Can't we at least give them a little discomfort before they die?"

"Yeah, but we have to make sure they don't hurt too much. If it's at the point where they prefer death, then we've gone too far. Not that I'd have any qualms about handing it to them!"

We were just heading down the stairs of the inn when a voice called out.

"Oh, you just got back. Are you heading out again?"

It was the inn's owner, the landlady.

I was considering how to respond when Minnalis opened her mouth.

"Yes! Master and I are heading out on a date!"

"M-Minnalis?!"

She calmly took my arm as I blinked at her in shock. Then she brought her head close to my ear and said in a low whisper, "Master, I think it would make for a better deterrent if we appeared to be intimate. After all, slaves can still be traded away if their master wishes. Better for me to seem like your favorite thrall with whom you wouldn't part for all the gold in the world."

"Mm... I guess you have a point..." I glanced over at her face, but it betrayed not a shred of emotion.

Not a shred. Just making sure you got that.

So wasn't this going to have the opposite effect? It's going to look like I, the master, forced an innocent slave girl into acting as my lover. How cringe is that?

"Minnalis, smile. Even if it's an act. If it's too embarrassing, then you don't have to hold on to my arm—just smile, for god's sake!!"

The landlady's eyes glazed over slightly as if she were witnessing something very sad. *Minnalis, please stop with the poker face! I'm begging you.*

"Whatever. Let's just go, Minnalis."

"M-Master?"

Now it was her turn to be puzzled. It was already too late to clear up the misunderstanding, so I just wanted to get out of there as soon as possible. I never thought there'd be an ambush waiting for me. That landlady was going to have to wrong idea forever now.

When I thought about being subjected to her pitiful gaze again, I wanted to cry. Not pee my pants, though.

By the time Zuily, Dot, and Terry finally arrived back at their inn, they were all reaching their limits and collapsed into their respective beds, snoring loudly until evening.

It was no surprise. Now that the excitement of catching the Oral

Rabbit and their second wind had worn off, exhaustion was starting to set in. For the past few days, they had been out hunting orcs, and then there was the rabbit hunt, the pub crawl, and now the argument with those newbies. Reaching their rooms at last had triggered a wave of exhaustion they simply could no longer resist.

Once they finally shook free of the shackles of drowsiness, the party gathered at their usual pub and raised one more glass to the capture of the Oral Rabbit.

"This is another fine mess you've gotten us into, Zuily."

The sun was still up, and there was a sprinkling of customers at the bar, as Dot interrogated Zuily over tankards of cheap ale.

"Eh, wossat?"

"Obviously, he means those kids," Terry replied, snacking on a little stir-fry as he enjoyed his drink. "Isn't this a bit of a duff job at our age? A D-rank party should be after more substantial prey than goblins."

Suddenly, Zuily burst out laughing. "Pfft! Ah-ha-ha-ha-ha!"

"Hmm? Did I say something funny?" asked Terry.

"Who knows?" said Dot, and two of them just stared at her in confusion.

"Ah, sorry, I thought I'd already told you. It's not a duff job. Far from it. I'd say we're probably looking at a few gold at least. It might even be our most substantial prey yet. The nose knows."

Terry and Dot leaned in closer, grinning.

"Oh, for real? Should be able to get some decent grub with that. Even with the Oral Rabbit, we only got enough to pay off half our bar tab."

"Gold, eh? That would be nice... There's a magic item I've had my eye on for a while..."

"Terry, always going on about your magic items. How about you try buying a woman fer a change, hmm?" advised Zuily, grinning.

Terry shrugged. "You two know that prostitutes aren't my thing."

"Yeah, you'd rather have a girl who kicks and screams," said Dot. "I don't see the appeal, myself. Isn't it annoying if she fights back?"

"That's the best part. Besides, you can hardly talk, neck-lover. You've got a rather weird fetish yourself."

"...Did you guys forget there's a lady at this table?" asked Zuily. "You both sound like sickos to me."

""Says the woman who enjoys torturing other women to death!"" "Touché."

Their uncouth laughter echoed around the room. In a bar at this hour, they were hardly out of place. Their laughter disappeared among those of the other patrons, and nobody could hear what they were saying.

"So which one's the target?" asked Dot. "The dumbass who started the whole thing? Or the skinny boy with a sword and his slave girl companion?"

"The dumbass. His staff is quite the artifact. He must be some noble's stock, probably pretty low in the pecking order if he's come all this way without a retainer. I'm betting he was disowned for being useless, and they gave him that staff to send him his way."

"He did seem to talk an awful lot about himself. I could very easily see a noble displaying that level of foolishness," noted Terry.

"And that kid with the slave girl seemed awfully polite as well," said Dot. "He must be related to some rich bigwig or be a noble's bastard son."

"He's a no-go," argued Zuily. "Wasn't carrying anything of value. He still has to die, so might as well have a little fun with that Lagonid slave of his while we're at it."

"Oh, sounds good," said Dot. "Make sure you let me have a go before you break her, boss."

"Would you let me go first?" asked Terry. "That's when you get the best screams."

The party let out another round of sleazy guffaws. Similar conversations were in progress all around the bar. Amid all the noise of revelry, not a single person overheard their conversation.

Not a single *person*.

"Squeak, squeak."

Only a mouse, hiding in the shadows beneath the tables.

On the body of that mouse glowed a strange magical mark. A Control Brand.

"Ha, I knew it. They are trash."

I had come out to the forest with Minnalis to survey the location of our battle in advance, and the mouse I had sent to spy on Zuily's party had brought me some useful information.

Of course, it was no ordinary rodent. It was a monster known as the Small Mouse that I had subjugated using the Monster's Blade of Hatching.

While the Small Mouse was technically a monster, in terms of combat ability it was no different from a regular mouse, and they littered the streets of big cities posing no particular threat.

The Monster's Blade of Hatching wasn't shaped like a sword. The guard and hilt looked normal enough, but the blade resembled an unripe flower bud. It allowed me to control any monster so long as its level was lower than the sum total of all my stats (not including HP and MP), divided by 100. The maximum number of monsters I could control at once was equal to my max MP divided by 100, and I could also store them inside some sort of magical pocket dimension within the blade itself. Last, controlling a monster allowed me to see through its senses.

I had captured Mouse #1 here as a test of my ability, but it turned out more useful than I'd expected. It couldn't understand, much less speak, any human language, but I could at least communicate "yes" and "no" using gestures. Since it was so small, I didn't even have to keep taking out and putting away the Monster's Blade of Hatching in order to store it in that mysterious space.

I could see what it saw, hear what it heard, and it could go nearly anywhere as long as there was a gap big enough for it to fit through. It was truly the perfect spy. And I had sent it out to monitor Zuily's party as a sort of test run.

"Hmm? What's that, Master?"

"I just got a report from Mouse #1. They're having a disgusting conversation."

"Can you let me listen in as well?"

"Hmm? Let you listen? Well, I haven't tried, but the Holy Sword of Retribution always keeps a magic channel open between us. I imagine we could set it up so you could tune in if we wanted to, but I wouldn't advise it. I really don't think you want to hear this."

I shrugged. Minnalis didn't appear to like my response.

"That's not very nice, Master. I may be your slave, but I'm also your partner in crime. I'm not saying you can't keep secrets, but you really don't need to worry about me. What would you do if I were to find out only after killing them that they hadn't suffered enough?"

"O-okay, settle down."

She stared right into my face. But I had to agree with what she was saying.

"Fine, okay then."

I tried linking up our magical channels so Minnalis could listen to what Mouse #1 was hearing. There was an electrifying, almost impossible to describe sensation, but it seemed to have worked.

Zuily's party were still engaged in their repulsive conversation. I could forgive some tactless utterances made in the grip of liquor, but the sorts of things they were saying were beyond that. It made me want to murder them on the spot.

Minnalis listened in with an impenetrable visage, but I could almost see the air around her shimmering with her fury.

Well, we couldn't stand around listening to them forever. It was time to get on with the inspection. Just as I thought that, Minnalis severed the connection. She looked at me with a smile worthy of the Virgin Mary.

"Master, tomorrow is going to be so much fun, isn't it?"

"...Y-yeah."

Even I was a little perturbed by her daunting smile.

The next day. After eating another similarly iffy breakfast, I left the inn with Minnalis. We didn't need to be up so early today, so it was a decent while after sunrise, and the town had already come alive.

In a town where people gathered from across the country, many stores were already starting to open around sunrise, and most traders were active by midday, such as hawkers flaunting their dubious wares on the street, novice merchants trying to turn a profit, and shopkeepers selling bargains in their secondhand stores.

Unlike in Japan, people in this world had no way of telling the exact time, so they relied on their internal clocks and the position of the sun to make rough estimates. And yet somehow, the shops all opened at the same time day after day after day. It was very strange.

Although I suppose I don't have a watch, so I can't check.

Today's battle would start at the east gate. It wasn't far from the inn, but there were a lot of shop stalls along the way. As much as I wished to sample some of the wares, we had no time to waste, so we walked straight to the place we had agreed to meet. However, there was already someone there.

"Hmm, I thought we would be the first ones," I muttered.

We were still a ways off, so he hadn't noticed us, but we could make out Hansel standing by the gate. He was speaking to a guard at the checkpoint. His glorious blond hair was easy to pick out, even among this crowd—in this world, they all had wacky hair colors.

"Did you want to be first, Master?" asked Minnalis.

"No, not really. It's just not what I expected."

Hansel didn't really seem like the kind of person to be overly keen about making his appointments.

I suppose I was also a little disappointed since I was going to have to go talk to him now and somehow resist the urge to strangle him to death on the spot. There would be enough of that today as it was.

"Well, the longer we starve, the better lunch will taste. Come on, let's go," I urged.

"Yes, Master!"

When we got a little closer, Hansel seemed to recognize us and bounded over, looking somewhat relieved.

"Morning all! You're running late. I thought I'd come to the wrong place!"

"Late? I thought we were a little early," said Minnalis. Most adventurers went out hunting a little later. Besides, all we had said was to meet before noon, so there was no "early" or "late" about it.

"What are you talking about? You were far earlier yesterday. And I'd ask you not to address me, slave. In fact, it's probably best you don't stand too close. I don't want your beast stench getting on me."

Hansel complained as if it were what he was born to do. He twisted up his face as he looked at Minnalis, and it was clear he had already labeled her as someone far below him.

It was a gaze I had been subjected to many times when the world had turned against me.

It was a gaze Minnalis had been subjected to many times by the people of her village.

It was a gaze that seemed to be the same wherever you went in this disgusting world.

"..."

"Anyway," he said, "about today. Why on earth did you retire early last night? We didn't get to practice our formations!"

"...What?"

While I fought to keep the rage from showing on my face, Hansel brought up something else. It was so sudden, I didn't quite realize what he meant.

"I said, we didn't get to practice our formations. How are we supposed to act efficiently as a party if we don't even know each other's abilities?"

Hansel wore a face like he was explaining all of this to a particularly dim-witted child.

All the thoughts in my head suddenly froze. Why did he think he was just going to be able to join our party? His skull must have been full of stuffing. As I reeled in shock, Hansel took that to mean I had no response. With some sort of proud look on his visage, he continued.

"Well, all we have to do is have you two distract the enemy so they don't come near me while I'm preparing my spells. Ah, but don't stray too far from me, got it? I haven't got the fine-tuning down yet, and the slave aside, I wouldn't want to be responsible for getting *you* caught in the cross fire."

...So basically you want us to act as your meat shields, is that it? What a stand-up guy.

Having us act as decoys was one thing, but this squirt basically just said he wouldn't care if he hit Minnalis by mistake. Logically, I could follow his reasoning, but emotionally, I had lost it.

"…" The sentiment on Minnalis's face, however, vanished almost instantly. She'd been relying on that skill of hers a little too much lately. I'd have to warn her about it later.

Ahhh, I just want to crush his stupid little face in my hands.

My feelings finally caught up with me, like a stove heating up the box containing my heart.

Hansel's behavior was not at all strange for the son of an aristocrat. By the time they grew up, they would no doubt have gained a modicum of humility. That was right for this world.

But I no longer cared about what was right and wrong. I'd tried that the first time.

I didn't want to think about it ethically. I didn't care if there were reasons why he was like that.

The only thing that mattered was how it made me feel.

"Minnalis, it's a little early, but let's preheat the oven," I whispered.

"Yes, Master!"

I didn't have to hold back.

I just had to wait. Just a few hours.

And once we'd finished the preparations, we could begin the banquet.

…I will make sure you feast on despair before you die.

While Minnalis hung her head in mock shame at Hansel's words, I watched a grin spread across her lips. Her emotions had become too much for the Iron Mask skill to conceal.

…Did my saying we could begin make you that happy, Minnalis?

Ahhh, what am I saying? Of course it did.

I know because we feel the same joy, the same pleasure.

Her mana started to take on an ominous hue.

"…So do you understand now why you should be impressed with me?"

"Oh yes, sir. Very much so."

While Minnalis worked her magic, Hansel seemed quite oblivious, instead rattling off all the spells he'd learned and what was so great about them. Minnalis obviously had no interest and kept her responses perfunctory. We could easily confer among ourselves while Hansel was enraptured with his speech, but I decided it would be best to let Minnalis concentrate for now.

"Indeed you should be. But that's not all! Heed my words, for one day my name shall be known throughout the kingdom—nay, throughout all the lands…!"

"…*Corrupting Needle.*"

And with those words, Minnalis's spell was complete. The weapon made of her hatred flew through the air, all but invisible to everybody else.

"Hmm? What's that? A bug?"

Hansel's loud mouth finally stopped moving. He put his hand to his neck, but there was no mark. Or rather, there was, but it was far smaller than a bug bite.

Corrupting Needle was a spell Minnalis had invented that, as the name implied, created a tiny needle out of frozen venom. It combined the poisons she made with Intoxicating Phantasm and an ice needle produced with the help of her relatively high affinity for ice and dark magic. We'd hit upon the idea in conversation together after leaving the capital and had managed to find the time to develop the spell on the way. It was difficult to control, but because of its small size and the minuscule amount of mana contained within it, it was almost impossible to detect with physical or magical senses. It melted immediately after poking a hole in the target, whereupon the poison entered the body. However, the icicle itself was not particularly strong and could be blocked by all but the weakest armor. Given the tendency of beastfolk magic to disintegrate over long distances, the spell was quite limited in its use and not nearly as versatile as we had hoped.

The ability to infect an unaware target, however, more than made up for its shortcomings. We only had one day. It was very important that no one catch on to what we were up to until it was too late.

"Oi, oi, what's all this? You got here early."

As if on cue, Zuily and her gang showed up.

"Didn't fancy making your elders wait? That's awfully considerate of you. Maybe if you grovel on the floor and lick the dirt off my boots, I'll let you go!"

It was painfully obvious she would do no such thing. I could see in her eyes, as they greedily passed between Hansel's staff and Minnalis, that she was merely taunting us. But Hansel couldn't. He flew into a rage, foolishly taken in by Zuily's insults.

"You got some nerve! As if I would ever stoop to such lowly behavior!"

"Oh, really?" replied Zuily, shrugging her shoulders in an exaggerated display of disinterest. "In that case, I guess we'd better get started."

"Just you wait! I'll have you all weeping before me!"

"Heh. I'd like to see you try. You should be more worried about lettin' the goblins get the better of you. It's happened to adventurers before."

"Wha—? Who in their right mind would lose to a goblin?"

"You never know in this business. You could be alive one minute, and dead the next. Surely you knew that, right?" said Zuily, chortling as she showed her plate to the checkpoint guard and passed through the gate.

The south gate, where we had arrived in town, was almost entirely overrun by the bushes and trees of the forest, but in contrast, the east entrance opened onto a vast green plain. After traveling northeast for some time, we arrived at a sprawling forest at the base of some small foothills. The six of us—me, Minnalis, Hansel, Zuily, Dot, and Terry—traveled mostly in silence until we arrived.

"All right. The match will last until sunset. Then return to the guild, make your report, and wait for the other team to arrive. If either team doesn't make it back to the guild by sundown, they forfeit."

"Okay, I get it already! Let's get a move on! With me on your team, we can't lose! Ah-ha-ha-ha!!" Hansel shouted.

Nice, looks like the poison is beginning to take effect.

Minnalis's poison started by absorbing the mana of its host, so the first symptom to display itself was MP drunkenness. It'd be only another hour, maybe two, before Hansel was completely incapacitated.

The boy leaped off into the forest with a cheer, and Minnalis and I walked after him. The plan was to break off from him and head after Zuily's party, but getting him to agree to that sounded like a pain, so we stayed with him for the time being. In any case, soon enough, it wouldn't matter. He'd be lying dead on the forest floor.

I glanced furtively over at the other party and watched Zuily and her friends disappear into the forest in another direction. Even now, she was watching us hungrily, her eyes clouded with greed.

"Haah…haah…haah…"

It was hot. How long ago had we entered the forest? It seemed like at least a minute, and yet it felt like no time at all.

This was strange. Something was wrong.

My body felt like it was burning. Was it heatstroke? My mind faltered. All I was doing was walking, but it felt as if I were moving through water.

…Dammit! Why now, of all times?

I pushed my aching joints onward. I knew there was no way I could win the match in this state, and yet I couldn't possibly give up and return to town without having slain a single goblin. It would be a disgrace.

…Goblins prioritize weakened opponents. If we run into one, it'll come after me, no doubt.

I looked up ahead. Somehow, the other two had gotten ahead of me. When did that happen? They looked fine. Whatever I had, it seemed like it was not affecting those two.

Looks like I've got no choice but to resort to plan B.

I may have been losing my mind, but I could still cast spells. If it came to a fight, I'd use a Fireball to hobble these two. Then the goblins would come after them, and I could finish them all off with Fire Lance. After that, all I'd have to do was collect all the ears and return to town. I could blame my loss on this illness; it'd still be impressive how many I'd managed to kill in this state.

It's not a very pretty method. As a noble, I don't want to rely on it. But…

This was about something more important. My pride.

I may have lost my status when I was chased out of the family, but I could still distinguish myself on merit. I could become an A-rank adventurer and establish my own house.

No, I will. I'm a noble. My father and my brothers may have laughed at me before, but we'll see who's laughing when I'm the one on top!!

That's right. I was a noble. And as one, I couldn't allow myself to face such shame on my very first mission. It was only natural that I exploited those two for my benefit. After all, what else were commoners for? Wait… Wasn't that boy an aristocrat? Well, it didn't matter. He had cast away his nobility the moment he took on a beastfolk for a slave.

Dammit, where are they? Where are the goblins?

I was really struggling now. I'd been taking stamina potions, but they didn't seem to help.

Then, suddenly, the two walking in front of me stopped in their tracks.

"Hey, Minnalis, you think we should get started?"

"Oh yes, Master. He's looking so pitiful now. I think it's about time."

"Hey, what are you two babbling about?" I asked, failing to conceal the anger in my voice.

But they didn't respond. Instead, they started moving again. This time, at a brisk pace.

"H-hey! Slow down! We have to move more carefully in the depths of the forest! What if we get ambushed by goblins?"

They were breaking an inviolable rule of adventuring. Never let your guard down in a monster's territory, especially when visibility was bad. I had to stop them. I shouldn't even have been raising my voice, but I hadn't the time to worry about that. If they went any faster, I wouldn't be able to keep up. I couldn't allow myself to be left alone in the forest in the state I'm in.

If I wanted, I could probably still put up a monster-repelling ward and make my way safely back to town, but I couldn't. My pride wouldn't allow it.

"Hey, wait! I said, wait!"

I called desperately after the pair, but they didn't stop, and soon they disappeared from view.

"Haah...haah...haah..."

I tried to gather my breath and look around, but there was no sign of them.

What now...? Should I go after them? Perhaps I should head back... No, what am I thinking? I couldn't possibly do something so shameful!

Thoughts whirled in my mind. My body sagged. As I shook my

head to remove those cowardly thoughts, suddenly I spotted a figure in the corner of my eye.

"Hmm! Ah!"

Almost as quickly as it appeared, it was gone. But it was that disgusting slave girl. I was sure of it. She couldn't have gotten far. I called out after her.

"H-hey! I'm over here! Wait for me!"

Calm down. Think. They need you. They can't win the match without your spells. There's no way they'd leave you behind.

I gripped my beloved staff and shouted as loudly as I could muster.

"Can't you hear me? I'm here! Right here!"

The staff I'd stolen from my house when I left had now become my walking stick as I climbed up the hill toward where I'd seen the figure.

"Dammit, have I lost her again?!"

I looked around once more. There was nobody there. Not a trace. The forest was silent. Still and cold. A piercing frigidity, like it was trying to get rid of me.

Then, just as I was about to give up, I saw the figure again at the edge of my vision. Again I chased after it, and again I lost track of it. Again. Again.

"Grrrhh! Damn it all! What the hell is wrong with those two?!"

They were laughing at me. They were laughing at me. They were all laughing at me!!

The heat and rage boiled my brain until I could no longer think. Then, after so many games of hide-and-seek, I finally arrived at a small garden.

"Haah...haah...haah... Wh-where am I...?"

It was a secret place, nestled among the trees, filled with a rare variety of flower with pale petals.

"What weedy-looking plants. Not an ounce of dignity in them."

"Hmm. So that's what they look like to you."

"Huh?"

Before I could turn around to face the voice, something nudged me slightly in the back.

"Hmm?"

Like a blade of ice, a chill ran up my spine, a freezing wave that flushed all the heat and anger from my body in an instant. It was a coldness I had never felt before in my life, and its spectral chill dominated me. Unable to keep my footing, I toppled to the ground. As I did, I turned and saw the man's face.

"Eek! Aargh?!"

He was not the man I'd met. His wicked smile turned me to stone. The feeling of the earth as I collided with the ground was so, so distant.

"Now, you'd better make the most of that feeling. This is the last chance you'll have to feel anything."

"Agh...wh...what...gah..."

My instincts acted before consulting with my rational mind, and I pressed my hands into the ground to rise to my feet. It felt as if it were all happening so very far away. Before I could even stand up, the man kicked me down once more.

Then, as I rolled along the ground, the sensation of the ground beneath my body disappeared.

"Guh..."

My stomach rose into my chest, then as I hit the ground again, it knocked the wind out of me. I was at the bottom of a deep hole, too deep to crawl out of unaided. Even the sun's rays, high in the sky as it was, did not reach me down here. The soil here was damp, like after the rain.

It was like it was my grave.

""..."""

Looking up out of the pit, I saw them standing over me. The man and the woman. When I first met him, I had thought him unimportant, with the only thing about him worthy of note being his striking black hair.

Having a slave girl had been a good sign. It meant he was of high birth. From a purely personal standpoint, I thought of him as a fellow noble.

But it was simply unacceptable for his thrall to be a beastfolk. Even if his family disowned him, even if he was forced to scrape together a living with his own two hands, to partner up with a foul beast was the same thing as discarding his pride. I knew then that we could never work together.

That's why this was always going to be a one-off. They were useful to me, for now, and if I needed to be rid of them, I could do so easily.

They were my pawns.

"Why are you glaring at me like that…? Why are you glaring at me like that?!"

But his eyes. It was like I had no value whatsoever.

"My, what a loathsome dullard. I simply cannot believe you are my own flesh and blood."

"What rotten luck I had to be stuck with a brother like you! Just go off and hide in a corner somewhere."

"Stop it…! Don't look at me like that!!"

The heat whittled away at my strength, and eventually, even that was sucked away by the chill. Though my body no longer listened to me, it burned with fervent indignation.

"You bastards, you bastards, you bastards! You're laughing at me! You're all laughing at me!!"

All of them! My father, my brother, and now these two!

"I'm a noble! You understand? I'm better than you! And I won't be put out by the likes of you!!"

My mana swelled, spreading through my body and blasting off the fetters of my weakened state.

"O ball of raging flame, heed my wrath! Take my mana and give my fury form! Let my incandescent rage reduce all who oppose me to ash! *Fireball!!*"

My anger unleashed a wave of mana from my body, and my staff amplified it to untold levels. I was only barely able to keep the spell under control. The flames roared like an unruly tiger.

"Ha…ha-ha! Die! Burn to ashes!!"

The blazing orb leaped from my hands to obliterate all in its path. *Yes! They're toast!*

It was on course for a direct hit. They'd never be able to dodge it in time.

…Or so I thought.

"Ahhh, what tepid flames."

All it took was a brush of his hand. He didn't even have to try. Just a flick of his wrist, and the flames were gone.

"…Huh?"

I couldn't believe what I was seeing. That was my prized spell. It was the most powerful attack I'd ever produced in my life.

Why? Why, why, why, why, why?!

"Waaaaaaarghhh! *Fireball!!*"

Hurry! Hurry!

I didn't even know why I was hurrying. My body simply obeyed my instincts.

"*Fireball… Fireball… Fireball…! Fireball!!* Wraaaaarrrgh!!"

I no longer cared about efficiency. I just put in just enough mana as was necessary to hold the form of the spell.

"They're pale," commented the man.

I'd lost control, but out of all the incantations I was hurling, one was sure to hit.

"Wh-what are you?"

But they didn't.

"And fragile," he continued.

Without even offering even an ounce of resistance, he snuffed all my spells out.

"WHAT ARE YOU?!"

"But most of all," he said, "they're tepid."

Last shot.

I squeezed out all my mana, the last of my MP, and poured it into one final Fireball. The spell to decide my fate.

Only for that man to crush it in the palm of his hand.

"Yet even flames as cold as these can still rekindle the fires of my heart."

"Aaagh! Why…? You… You're a monster!" I managed to get out in a trembling, quavering voice.

He hadn't even done anything to me, but the feeling of being trampled on, of my pride and joy being torn apart, was too much to bear. Even as my body slowly succumbed to heat and exhaustion, my mind was annoyingly as sharp as ever, and it never let that feeling go.

"You think?" he asked. "Well, you can blame your future self for angering *this* monster."

His black eyes looked down at me.

"To be honest with you, I wasn't sure I was going to kill you guys. After all, you weren't the ones who betrayed me, and logically, I can't really fault your behavior. So on one side of the scales, I could have done nothing."

"Wh-what are you…?"

"I guess that just means my scales must be busted. Because there's no way this is the right thing to do. This is just petty revenge, like a child who throws a tantrum when he doesn't get what he wants. But still…"

They were the eyes of the dead. Like a broken puppet missing a critical piece. A pair of vacant eyes. And deep within, a fire so dark I couldn't even see what was burning.

"I thirst. I thirst so bad I can't take it. And I know, in my head, I'm overthinking it, that I've just got a persecution complex, but it's no use. Every time I look at you, I can still smell the burning flowers, still feel the garm's cold dead body... I can't escape it!"

The dead man smiled.

He smiled in reverence of a thirst so black I do not even know what it was for.

"So I don't care anymore if I'm no longer a hero. All I see in the mirror is an ugly, vile, coarse man. A revenant emerging from the depths of the swamp."

His voice seemed stained with blood. The dead man took out some kind of flask from his pouch and poured its contents into the hole.

"Blah! Wh-what is this? Oil...?"

The liquid got in my eyes, and I couldn't clearly see what it was, but it felt slippery and clung to my skin, and its unmistakable smell filled my nostrils.

"Tell me, didn't you feel the pain? Or did the MP drunkenness and the poison make it too hard to tell?"

"What?"

"Look at your hand. *It's melting.*"

"Wh-what?"

I glanced down. I didn't even have the time to question what he meant.

The enduring heat. The exhaustion. The sudden loss of MP. The damp hole. I had thought a few drops of sweat to be nothing surprising.

"What the hell is this?! Why? Why?"

But it wasn't sweat. It was just as the dead man said.

"Waaaaaaaaaaaaaarrrrrghhhh!!!"

…Something else was dripping down my fingers, like molten wax. Something that definitely wasn't sweat.

"It's melting! Like a candle! Aaaargh! Grrrrrgghh!"

Even if my mind didn't know what that liquid running down my hands was, my instincts did. It was my own body. A patchwork glob of pale skin, pink flesh, and red blood.

As soon as I saw it and understood, I felt pain like my skin was being flayed off.

"Ha-ha-ha! Like a candle, he says! Now that's a nice image! That's exactly right. Your flesh is now like wax. You won't burn, you'll melt. Nice and slowly."

His voice was soft, like melting venom. The dead man held a single match.

"Grh…! Rggh.! No… Stop!"

"Burning to death would be too good for you. You're going to watch your own body dribble away. You're going to feel the heat roast your body until your last moments. And then you're going to die."

"Stooooooopppppp!!"

Then I saw the dead man's lips break into a chilling, ghoulish smile…

…and the match tumbled from his fingers and spiraled gently into the pit.

The oil erupted into roaring flame.

"Graaaaaargh! Aaargh! It's burning! Gyaaaaaagh!"

It burns! It burns! It burns!!

Why? Why? Why was this happening?!

My body dripped away as the flames wrapped around me.

"I suppose you want to know why I'm doing this to you, don't you? Well, good. Now you know how I felt. I wanted to know why it all happened that night. I wanted to know so, so much."

"Graaaaagh! Aaaaaaghh! AAAAAAAAAAAAAA!!"

"What's the matter?! Where are your fancy spells now, huh?"

Even the air I breathed in was searing my lungs. The raging flames heated the air, and I was melting, inside and out. The inferno caused bits of my body to puddle and pool on the ground.

"Here, Master! I fetched some more oil!"

"Cheers, Minnalis! Here you go, have a refill!"

"GAAAAAAAAAAGH?! Aaagh! Grrrgh!"

"Hee-hee! I'll help out as well!"

"Yeah, come on. Quickly now, before he melts! Ah-ha-ha-ha-ha!!"

"Gwaaaaaagh! Hrg! Gruuuueeeehhh?!"

The two sloshed oil on me from above, as if playing with me. Each time a torrent of fuel came raining down, the flames burst with new life and liquefied another part of my body.

"Bbblgh! It huuuuurts! Help… Help meeeee!!"

"No way. After all, when I pleaded with you to stop, did you listen to a word I had to say?"

My melting face blocked my mouth, making it difficult to breathe. Both the outside and inside of my body were turning to mush. The pain and heat were so unbearable I thought it better to drop dead right away and get it over with. But only my body was melting. My mind was still sharp, and I could feel in excruciating detail the sensation of my form getting smaller and smaller.

"Come on, come on, come on! Suffer! Scream! I want everything you burned that day to hear you! Melt! Crumble! Wither in pain!"

My body was falling to pieces. I watched as what had once been a limb slowly dissolve into a puddle on the ground, as if mocking me. My arms fell from their shoulders, my legs descended into puddles, and my face blistered and bubbled until I could no longer see.

"Gbbh! Gh! Bh…"

My ears and nose had long since melted away, but I could still feel the pain. Then, finally, my eyelid flesh seared over my eyes.

"Ah-ha-ha-ha!! Here's the last flask of oil! Let's see a marvelous pyre!"

My right eye was already gone. With my world cut in half, the last things I saw were the orange flames and the pure white sun.

And silhouetted therein, the form of the dead man, looking down on me with a twisted smile.

In the next moment, everything went black. But the heat and pain never vanished until the moment my consciousness was obliterated.

"Man, burning things never gets old."

The garm must have suffered a similar fate, trapped inside that church. Or perhaps it was crushed to death in an instant by falling rubble. I'll never know.

"…If I could make a wish, I'd like for it to have died a quick and painless death," I said.

The moisture in Hansel's body made a crackling sound as it burned. It was the same sound as the trees had made in my past life.

"Right. One down, three to go. Let's go, Minnalis, we've still got a lot to do."

I took in the smell of burning flesh one more time before rising to my feet.

"Yes, Master."

"You're next, Zuily, Dot, Terry. I'll show you the terror you only get to feel once in life."

This was only the first act. I'll kill you all. Kill you all. Kill you all. Every last one of you.

I'll drag you down to the depths of hopelessness and despair.

Later, an adventurer happened upon a bizarre sight in the forest. In a small clearing, in the center of a circle of flowers, someone had dug a large hole. Within the hole was the unmistakable stench of burning flesh, and the earthen walls of the pit had been charred black. An investigation by the town of Golet determined that due to the nature of the trap, it was likely that bandits or possibly Redcaps were to blame. However, a body was never produced, and soon enough, the incident faded from public memory.

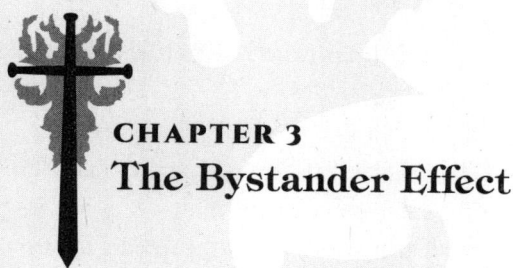

CHAPTER 3
The Bystander Effect

"Whoopsie-daisy. Look, Dot, there's one over there. Don't let it get through."

As Zuily cleaved a goblin in half with her two-handed broadsword, another slipped past her guard and made a beeline for Terry in the rear. Dot, however, was quick to react to her words and stood in the goblin's path.

"I got it already! Terry!"

He swung his sword down at the goblin, but the monster blocked the first attack with its club, a crude weapon made of some bit of tree it had found lying around. With his second blow, Dot put some distance between himself and the creature.

"Got it in my sights!" Terry launched a bullet of ice at the lone goblin. The creature couldn't dodge, and as the man's spell blew a hole in its chest, it let out a single strained cry that sounded like a frog being squashed. Meanwhile, Zuily mowed down a final goblin with her greatsword and brought the battle to a close. After severing their ears for trophies, the three of them regrouped.

A few hours had passed since they'd entered the forest. The sun was at its peak, and the number of goblins Zuily's team had defeated had just reached double digits.

"We've managed to do better than expected," observed Zuily. "What say we break for lunch?"

"*Phew*, finally," said Terry with a sigh.

"You've got no energy, Terry," scolded Dot. "I spotted a clearing up ahead while I was scouting. Let's move there."

Dot led his party to the clearing, and they all picked a spot on the ground and sat down. Then Dot produced some meat jerky and rye bread from an old sack.

"So how come we ain't gone after the brat and his staff the moment we entered the forest? That's what we're really after, right?"

"Dot, you moron. We may as well let 'em hunt some extra goblins for us to take back with us. Besides, we have to stay out here awhile or the guild'll think something's fishy when we come back. We're still planning to stay in this town for a while, after all... Mng."

Zuily washed down her dry bread with a swig of water and tore into the hard meat with her teeth.

"Anyway, they can't have gone far. They gotta be back in town by sundown or they forfeit the match. Not only that, but you don't have to go deep into the forest to find a bunch of goblins."

"True, the encounter rate here does seem particularly high compared to other forests," noted Terry.

"Did ya not know?" Zuily asked. "A few years back, there used to be a village by the base of the mountains here. One day, stray demons possessed the townsfolk so they could stage an assault on the city of Elmia. In the end, it never came to that, but the villagers went mad from their possession and started lashing out at anything and everything, so the soldiers had to come and put 'em all to death."

"And what does that have to do with the high encounter rate? I don't see the connection."

"Just let me finish, will ya? Why do you always gotta skip over the fun stuff?" said Zuily, waving her water bottle at Terry. "So that village disappeared, and all the requests asking adventurers to come to this forest suddenly stopped. Until then, there were quite a few coming in from Elmia, too, but they all stopped as well."

"And then, as if to make matters worse, a *silly rumor* starts going around! And all the superstitious rookie adventurers who came here for experience stop showing up, too!"

"Hey, I'm the one tellin' this tale! Don't steal the show!" cried Zuily, bringing her fist down on Dot's head.

"Ow! You didn't have to hit me, boss!"

Ignoring his teary eyes, Zuily returned to her story.

"And so, apart from the guild's regular monster-slaying expeditions, adventurers stopped coming to this forest. Without anyone to cull the numbers, obviously that's gonna make the encounter rate go up."

"I see. And so what was this silly rumor?" Terry cocked his head as Zuily took another bite of her jerky.

"Terry, you should pay attention to more than just your magic items," warned Dot. "They said that the ghosts of those villagers still haunted this forest, and that if ya met one, you'd suffer a curse that can never be lifted. That's what kept people away."

Terry let out a brief sigh. "Good grief. Undead appearing is one thing, but ghostly curses? The imaginations of some people."

"Well, it wasn't just that rumor which kept people out. Even if you ignored it, the only monsters you can find in these parts are goblins and Green Boars. There ain't nothing worth the trouble of defeating, and even if you're just after experience, if you've got half a head, you'll stay away from this forest and pick somewhere less crowded. Plenty other places you can find goblins and Green Boars without being up to your neck in 'em."

Terry nodded in agreement.

"In fact, we're quite lucky those twerps picked this place. This way we can kill 'em without anybody finding out."

"In that case, shall we get it over with? My MP is starting to wane from these constant back-to-back battles. It'd be best to get it done after this short rest... I wish to see that beastfolk slave weeping and screaming as soon as possible, and since we're killing her right after, I have to make the most of it."

Terry began to laugh cruelly, and Dot joined in.

"After we kill the two guys, we'll have to find an abandoned lodge to have our fun," he said. "Don't want the monsters to catch us with our pants down, so to speak!"

"Aren't you two forgetting something? The staff's what's important! Also, if you break that girl before I get a chance to, I'll rip off the ones between your legs!"

""All right, all right!""

"Ugh, guys are all talk. You know we gotta take that kid out first, right? The other two fledglings'll be quaking in their boots after they see their partner die, so before they can act, we hobble that skinny punk's legs so he can't walk. Ah, I'd like to keep him alive, if you don't mind."

"Hmm? Why not kill him?"

Dot looked confused. It was Terry who answered his question.

"You just don't get it, do you?"

"What do you mean?"

""It'll be way more fun to see the look on that kid's face as his slave is defiled in front of him!!"" the other two both let out in unison, and then Zuily's boisterous laughter mingled with Terry's sly chuckles.

"Eh. I don't really see it. Seems like it'd be more annoyin' than anything else, to me. Oh well, if that's what you guys want, then I can't disagree."

"Wouldn't it be great if we could get her to betray her Master in return for her life?" suggested Zuily.

"Then how about we have that slave girl finish off that thin whelp for us? We can tell her we'll let her live if she does," added Terry.

"I like that sound of that. Buuut, she's probably been commanded not to defy her master, so I doubt it'll work."

"You two are twisted," said Dot. "Well, as long as you don't damage her neck, it's all good with me." This time it was he who shrugged his shoulders in resignation. He didn't really mind either way. Sure, it was dangerous to leave the punk alive, but he'd only just registered the previous day. He was a complete novice. What harm could he do? As long as they killed the mage kid first, the others would pose no threat.

"Right then, let's finish eating and head out."

It was only the scout, Dot, who was fast enough to raise a voice in response to what happened next.

"Whoa—"

But he was unable to warn his party in time. Even if all three of them had been on guard, the attack was so swift they would not have been able to react.

A paralytic mist was carried by the soft breeze and descended upon the three. In an instant, that semitransparent white mist immobilized the lot of them.

"Wh-what...? P-paralysis...?"

What the hell? A Paraz Moth? Why would it be here? No...their spores don't take effect this quickly...!

Then the mist vanished as quickly as it had appeared. It had already sunk in.

"Dammit... I can't move...!"

"B-boss! Th-this ain't good... I can't...move a muscle...!"

"Just...wait. I'll drink a healing potion... and then..."

Whether by her higher stats or just plain fortuity, Zuily could still move, albeit sluggishly. She forced her stubborn hand down to the pouch belt at her hip. Her arm moved excruciatingly slow, but at last she reached the detox potion she kept on hand for emergencies.

Dammit, move faster...!!

Taking care not to drop it, she slowly brought the potion up to her lips.

"All...right..."

As the potion came into view at last, that was when she heard it.

"Oh, my condolences! You were too slow!"

I descended on that place, like a demon stoking the fires of hell.

"Gaaaaaaaagh!!"

The glass of her vial shattered beneath my boot, and with my rage-filled stomp, I must have lacerated her hand as well, for red blood pooled out from under my foot and stained the earth.

"Hey, how does it feel to be thwarted so close to your goal? Just when you think, *Thank goodness, I'm nearly there*? How does it feel to have everything taken away from you and torn apart before your very eyes?"

"Grrrh! Arghhh!!"

"Huh, I guess you can't answer me, can you?"

I suppose some of the detox potion must have entered her bloodstream via the wounds in her hand and begun to counteract the numbness. Not enough so she could move again, but just enough so she could feel the pain in her hand.

"Master, it's not nice to steal my food before I get a taste."

"Hmm? Ah, sorry. It was just so perfect that I couldn't help myself."

I shrugged and lifted my shoe from her hand. My playful, taunting words were coming from above her head, where she couldn't see.

"That...voice...!"

Lying facedown on the ground, unable to move her neck, Zuily could see only as high as our waists. There was no way she would've forgotten my voice after only a few hours.

"What...are you doing...? Graaargh!!"

"This piece of trash is awfully loud, Master. It's harsh on my ears."

Minnalis trampled Zuily's hand even more brutally than I had done.

"Who did you say you were going to defile in front of whom, again? I can't believe the filth that comes out of your mouth, you roach."

"Grh! Gah! Aaaaargh!!"

The cruelty with which she trampled that hand was a testament to the extent of her anger. I could hear a crunching sound like gravel as she crushed it beneath her boot, a look of supreme disgust on her face.

"And I'm to beg for my life before you? Betray my master for you? ...Just how much are you willing to put me through before you're satisfied, huh?!"

"Y-you're... Ghah!"

Zuily tried to speak, but Minnalis kicked her in the jaw. Then she trampled on Zuily's other hand, and she let out another cry of pain.

"Do you dwo...habe any idea...whad you're doing...?"

Thanks to the antidote moving through her bloodstream, Zuily could still speak to some extent, even if she couldn't move.

"Huh? What's that supposed to mean, you fat sow?"

"Ugh!! Stop— Graaargh!!"

"What's wrong? Does your hand hurt? Hmm?"

"Stop! Graaaargh! Urghhhh!"

Now that Minnalis had lifted her foot from Zuily's right hand, it was my turn again. I crushed her hand beneath my boot for a while, listening to her screams.

"Now then, which of you said to have Minnalis kill me? It was you, wasn't it, third-rate archer?"

"Th...ird...rate...?!"

I peeked over at Terry, chuckling. His sharp glare made it clear what was on his mind.

"That's right. Third. Rate. To be honest, I'm surprised you've survived this long. It's a miracle, if you ask me."

"You think I'll...let you...? Gah! Gghh?!"

I kicked him over onto his back and launched my foot into his jaw just as Minnalis had done.

"Hey, does that hurt? Does it? Having to crawl around on the ground like a caterpillar while I talk shit about you? How does it feel? Come on, tell me!"

Smiling, I approached Terry, plucked the bow from his fingers, and snapped it in two before his eyes. As he glared up at me in indignation, I merely sneered back down at him and dropped my boot onto into his stomach.

"Stop... Please stop..."

After kicking him in the gut repeatedly, his mind finally snapped, and those words were all he could muster.

I'd had my fill and looked over at Minnalis. She was playing with Dot now, breaking down his will to resist.

"I don't know why the others keep you around if you can't even warn them of one measly ambush. And we were watching your battle, too. All you do is leave the killing to other people. What a worthless piece of trash. You know what they call people like you? Parasites. Oh, sorry, perhaps you're too stupid to understand that."

"Gr... Stop...this..."

Minnalis kicked Dot around on the ground, looking down at him with a sneering smile. Well, maybe "smile" wasn't the right way of putting it—she had lost none of her anger, and the rage was clear on her face as she beat him without mercy.

While he had showed resistance at first, Dot, too, gave in to the pain and eventually could manage nothing but weak groans. Perhaps we were rougher than we meant to be, but it's what they deserved. Their words earlier were like oil for our flame.

"So you were planning to kill us. Obviously, you considered the possibility that we would counterattack, right? You prepared yourself for this eventuality, didn't you? You've made your peace?"

I put a fair bit of mana into my aura and watched the faces of Zuily's party turn pale. It seemed they finally realized what kinds of people they were up against with. If they had still been thinking they could have fought back if only they hadn't been taken by surprise, then now I had finally shattered that last shard of defiance.

With their pride stripped from them, all they had left were pathetic whimpers.

"W-we were wrong! W-we'll make it up to you, just please, spare our lives—!"

"Whoops, sorry, it's a bit early for that," I said, cutting her off. "We're only just getting started. Don't start saying 'spare me' yet— this is just a warm-up. Minnalis!"

"Yes, Master!"

Minnalis nodded and used her Intoxicating Phantasm to create what we might call an anesthetic. A red-and-orange marbled orb of liquid appeared in her palm. It was about the size of a marble, too; a strong enough dose for the three of them. Unlike the numbing poison, this would only rob them of their sense of touch and immobilize them. They'd still be able to see, hear, and speak, but they would be unable to feel anything or move a muscle from the neck down.

So you can see, it wasn't quite like the anesthetic in our world.

"Now then, let's start the preparations. Master, could you help me administer the poison?"

"Sure."

"Wh-what are you—? Gwah!!"

I held open the mouths of Zuily's party as Minnalis poured the poison inside.

"Okay, it should take effect immediately. It's even stronger than that paralytic we just used, so it should override the effects and allow them to talk again."

Minnalis's mouth curved up into a crescent. It seemed the MP drunkenness was kicking in, and she was adopting her usual seductive behavior. This always happened when she made complex poisons with Intoxicating Phantasm, which required a lot of MP.

That smile sent a chill up my spine, but it also took my breath away. It was beautiful and terrifying all at once.

"Hee-hee-hee! Just you sit tight and wait! We'll show you a glimpse of the depths of hell!" exclaimed Minnalis. It was clear from the look on her face she was enjoying this from the bottom of her heart.

"All right, I suppose I should start getting ready, too."

Minnalis had already made her preparations. Now it was my turn. I would need two of my soul blades: the Monster's Blade of Hatching and the Fairy's Blade of Water.

First, I conjured up the former in my hand. If I was sloppy with my control while constructing a soul blade, then the mana would leak out, taking on a distinctive hue. This time, I thought that might add to the spectacle, so I let it happen. Tiny motes of black light danced in the air.

"Come forth with beastly voice. *Hatching Flower.*"

As I channeled my mana into the sword, red, pulsating veins

appeared along the green flower bud that acted as the blade. Then the bud grew black and purple splotches and swelled up, as Zuily's party looked on in horror.

"Wh-what the hell is that...?" asked Zuily.

"Hmm? Sorry, can't tell you that yet," I replied with a fake grin.

It seemed Minnalis's new poison had taken effect already, for while Zuily could not move a muscle otherwise, she could now speak normally. Terror and uncertainty were beginning to show on her face as she watched the Monster's Blade undergo its unsettling transformation. While her group couldn't guess what was going to happen, they could clearly tell it was going to be something very bad for them.

Then, with a *shriek*, the flower petals unfurled.

"Jarrllghhh!"

""""Grh!!""""

It was a shrill cry, inhuman, like glass scraping on a chalkboard. It wasn't particularly loud, but it took the three adventurers by surprise, and their faces froze in terror.

As for how I was handling it...

"Nnnrgghh. Master, I really hate that sound!"

"Minnalis... I said I'm fine."

She had just come from behind me and clapped her hands over *my* ears. We hadn't come across any good earplugs in town, so I told her to just plug up her own ears when the time came.

"Eh-heh-heh... That's no good, Master... I'm your slave...you should order me to serve you! Whee! Whee!"

"Ah! Stop it! Let go of me! Your breasts are touching me!"

"What do you mean, Master? I'm doing it on purpose!" Minnalis giggled. The MP drunkenness had unveiled her naked lust.

"Settle down for a bit."

"Aw. Don't I get a reward for being so good?"

"Rrrgh. Fine, but later. Just drink this."

In a motion I was getting used to, I pulled Minnalis toward me and forced an MP potion down her throat. All the while I was saying to myself, *It's just the MP drunkenness. It's just the MP drunkenness.* It seemed to be even worse than usual this time, but soon enough she would return to her usual self, I was sure.

"Wh-what the hell is wrong with these two?"

"I—I dunno…"

Terry and Dot, meanwhile, looked very confused. They couldn't understand us. They had no idea what was coming, and they were afraid. I could hear it in the particular quality of their voices. Zuily, meanwhile, was less interested in our conversation. Her thoughts were dominated by the sight of the creature emerging from my Monster's Blade of Hatching.

"Now, how are you feeling, Slimo?"

"Kupie!"

An oddly cute voice answered as Slimo the Slime emerged from the blade. Through the Control Brand, I could tell that it seemed to be in top condition. After ejecting Slimo, the flower of the Monster's Blade withered back into a bright green bud again.

"A…a slime?" asked Zuily in confusion.

"Yep, not a variant, nothing strong, just an ordinary slime," I replied. Indeed, it was nothing special. It had no eyes, no nose, no mouth, just a transparent blue body, like jelly. It was about the size of a balance ball, a little larger than average, but not enough to make it a variant. The only thing that distinguished it from a run-of-the mill monster was the Control Brand drawn in mana on the surface of its springy body.

Slimo wiggled on the ground, chirping its signature cry. I always wondered where its voice came from since it didn't have a mouth.

"All right, now, I know it's a lot I'm asking of you, but are you ready?"

"Kupie! Kuupie!!"

Leave it to me! it seemed to be saying. I gave it a good pat on the head…or, well, the top part of its body, anyway. Its skin felt cool and elastic. It was a pleasant sensation.

I dispelled the Monster's Blade of Hatching and conjured up the Fairy's Blade of Water in its place. The bladeless hilt was wrapped in a deep blue cloth.

"All right, I'm counting on you, Slimo!"

"Kupie!! Uu…ku!"

Slimo made a cheerful noise in response and, with what appeared to be a little bit of strain, split itself in two. I held my sword near one of the new Slimos and used its body to form its blade. It was about a tenth of the sword's normal size and composed of the same translucent blue as the slime itself.

"Wh-what? What are you trying to do?" asked Zuily.

"I wonder. What do you think?" replied Minnalis, chuckling in anticipation of what was to come.

"You'll find out soon enough," I said. "The preparations are complete. At my current level, it's quite difficult for me to maintain this blade for very long, so let's not waste any more time."

The corners of my lips curled up in a smile. First, I approached Zuily and held my sword up in my right hand.

"W-wait… Please, stop…"

"Oh, don't worry. You won't die. Yet."

Zuily's face twitched in terror. I sneered at her and cut off her head, then did the same with the other two.

"Oh, don't worry. You won't die. Yet."

The face I looked up at was plastered with psychotic joy. Out of the corner of my eye, I saw him raise his blue crystalline blade, and, as if in slow motion, I felt it cut into the back of my neck.

Dammit! I can't die here! Not to a punk like this!!

I felt my decapitated head rolling along the ground. Maybe it was because of that Lagonid girl's poison, but I didn't feel any pain. Even now, I could still see. I watched him cut off the heads of Terry and Dot as well.

I had heard that executed criminals could still move their mouths and blink for a few moments after their heads were removed. I guess that was true. However, it would only be a few more seconds before the specter of death consumed me.

I watched as he finished off the party members with whom I'd faced and overcome so many brutal struggles. Without the pain, my death didn't even feel real. All that was left was to await the…

"W…wait, what?! What's going on?!"

A second, two seconds, three seconds. Why wasn't I gone yet?

Had I not been decapitated after all?

"Wh-what the hell?! Didn't you cut off my head?"

"How is this happening?! I thought I was supposed to be decapitated…!"

I heard the bewildered voices of Dot and Terry. Out of the corner of my eye, I could see their heads rolling gently along the ground, and something covering the base of their necks where the blade had sliced through.

"Pff! Ah-ha-ha! Sorry, my bad! I guess you can't see too well!"

The kid's laugh gave me the chills. No sooner did I see his foot appear before my eyes than I felt a tug on my hair and rose into the air. When he brought me level with his own eyes, only then did I finally understand the state I was in.

"Wh-whaaat?! What the hell?!"

From here, I could see the ground below clearly. There lay *my own body*, twitching and oozing blood from its severed neck.

"What's happening?! Why am I...? You cut off my head! That's my body! Why am I still alive?!"

"Heh, pretty cool, eh? I had Slimo cover your neck when I cut off your head. It's keeping the blood pumping, taking in oxygen from the air, maintaining blood pressure, allowing me to keep you alive. See, it's even acting as your lungs and vocal cords, which is why you can still speak. And Minnalis's poison prevented you from dying from shock immediately."

"Huh? What are you talking about? Don't just talk gibberish—explain yourself!"

"Ahhh, well, I guess you wouldn't understand. Even Minnalis was confused when we tried it on a goblin."

"Maybe that's normal in your world, Master, but here, people die when they're killed! Severed heads that can speak are like something out of a horror story!"

"Well, it's not common in my world, either. Actually, it's *more* normal for this world, since you already have the undead and such."

"But the undead don't talk or breathe!"

"...That's true, they don't."

Once again, the damn kids were having another ridiculous conversation in front of us.

"Well, let's just say we've kept you alive from the neck up. Look, I'll show you."

He gave a dramatic shrug and placed my head on the rock where we had just been sitting. Then the sword he was holding melted into nothing, and he hoisted up Terry's and Dot's heads by their hair.

Their faces were frozen in expressions of shock. I was sure I was making the same face, too. I could see the transparent blue substance—a slime, apparently—covering our necks. Moving around and pulsating rhythmically within it was a muddy red fluid, which seemed to be our blood.

My head was spinning. It was like he'd turned us into monsters.

"You understand now? Come, I've prepared a little show. Not many people get to see this before they die."

But he was the true monster, playing with our lives, a bone-chilling smile on his lips.

He placed Terry's and Dot's heads alongside my own.

"Slimo!"

"Kupie!"

The slime responded to the kid's call, and slowly started creeping toward our bodies.

"Wh-whoa, hold on, what are you doing?"

I felt like I'd said that a million times today. The kid didn't answer. He just smiled as he petted the slime on the head, and said, in a voice devoid of emotion…

"Dinnertime."

"Kupie!"

"No…! Noooooo!!"

At that single word, the slime pounced forward as if it had been waiting and descended upon our bodies.

"Noooo!! Stop! Stooop! My body…!!"

There was a series of sickening crunches as the slime compressed our bodies. And it wasn't just me who screamed out in horror.

"Stop! Stop this at once!! If you lay another hand on our bodies, I'll…! D-do you know who we are?! Stop this at once, I said!!"

"Wh-what the hell, man…? This…is a dream!! Gyaha! Gyahaha! Yeah, it's a dream! It's gotta be! I mean, this don't make no sense!

There's no way this could all be really happening! Gyahahaha-haha!!"

It really seemed like a vision, like Dot said. A terrifying nightmare.

"Heh-heh-heh. Well, what do you think? This is a rare experience, I think, watching your own body be devoured while you're still alive. I do hope it's to your liking."

Just as the Lagonid girl said, we could see exactly what was happening inside the slime's transparent blue body. We heard the dull crunch of our bones snapping. I saw Dot's arm get mangled with a crack. I watched Terry's foot twist and break in two. I witnessed the armor being stripped off my torso, watched my belly burst open and my organs be squashed together like red meatballs.

And every time I watched part of my mangled body being torn out of shape, I felt something inside me crack.

"No… This can't be happening… It's not happening, it's not happening, it's not happening…"

Terry was the next to break after Dot. He just kept whimpering, "It's not happening" over and over again.

"Aargh! Please, just stop! We're sorry! We're sorry! Please, just stop…! No more…!!"

A strangled voice was all I could manage. My own body was being toyed with, mangled, while all I could do was watch. I was going to lose my mind.

I knew this was the end. But I didn't want to be driven mad before it happened.

"Hmm, pathetic. You're already giving up, and you haven't even felt any pain."

"Even the goblin was more fun to torture than you."

"Yeah."

Behind the laughing duo, the scraps of our bodies mixed and

swirled within the slime until it was no longer possible to guess whose was whose.

I didn't get it. I didn't get it. I just didn't get it.

Who *were* they? *What* were they? Why were they laughing? Why were they just having a friendly chat while I was in this state?

"*Kyupuh!*" After feasting itself on our bodies, the slime spat up a huge metal lump that had been our equipment.

"Grrrr! What did we ever do to you?!" I roared with fury, but the brat before me didn't appear unsettled in the slightest.

"Huh? What're you talking about? Don't get mad at *me*. You were going to rape Minnalis in front of me, weren't you? And then you were going to kill me."

"B-but, still. This is just too cruel…"

"Cruel? Surely you're joking. You thought if you were strong, you could get away with anything, and nobody would care as long as they didn't find out. Well, then you need to accept that if you're weak, anything can be *done* to you, and if people *do* find out, then they *will* care. This is just the natural consequences of your behavior, don't you think? Hey, I'm asking you a question."

"…"

"Don't sulk. This isn't cruel. If you're gonna live by the sword, then you ought to die by the sword. This is a fitting end for scum like you, don't you think?"

"A fitting…end…?"

"Listen, Zuily. You mustn't do bad things. They have a way of coming back to bite you."

"Tsk. Yeah, yeah. Whatever, you're always going on about this karma or whatever."

"That's right, karma. What goes around comes around. Remember that, and grow up into a good strong girl…"

*   *   *

Suddenly an old memory came to mind. A conversation with the village priest from when I was just a child.

I see, so this is karma.

These were all the bad things I've done coming back to bite me.

…So what?!

"No, no, no, no!!"

I don't want to die! I don't want to die! I DON'T WANT TO DIE!!

Not like this!!

Ever since I'd become an adventurer, I knew I would die by the side of the road somewhere. But I never expected anything this awful! This is just too much!

"Well, I suppose it's about time to say good-bye. Minnalis, Slimo, and I will take one each."

"Yes, Master!" cried the beastfolk girl as she reached into her item pouch, retrieving an old, rusted mallet.

"It's a dream, it's all a dream! A nice, lovely drea—"

"Bye-bye!"

"Gplh!"

There was the swish of the hammer in the air and a sickening splat from beside me. Dot's hot, sticky blood was plastered over the side of my face.

"Next, Slimo. Time for your dessert."

"Kyui!"

The kid's pet slime extended two feelers from its body.

"It's not happening. This *can't* be happening. It doesn't make any sense. It can't be happening, because...it just can't be— Blghf!"

The creature swallowed up Terry's head within itself. There was the dull snap of flesh and bone cracking, tearing apart. One of his eyeballs flew out of the slime's body and rolled along the ground, but the slime picked it up with a feeler and sucked it back inside like liquid through a straw.

"No...why is this happening...? Why? Why...? Gah!"

"That's what I asked myself all the time. It's what I screamed into the sky. *Why is this happening?* But you never answered me. So why should I answer you?"

The last thing I saw as my vision split in two was that punk's smile. Laughing with scorn, as though looking down in disgust on the entire world, even himself.

Ah, at last.

I'd finally finished them off.

"Master, are you crying?"

"Huh?" I brought my hand to my cheek. It was true.

"I wonder why. Ha-ha-ha... I dunno, but...I feel good. Really good. You feel it, too, don't you? I mean, you're crying as well."

"What?" She tapped her face gently, and sure enough, tears were streaming down her face.

As for why we were weeping, I didn't know.

It wasn't sadness, but it wasn't joy, either.

There was no pain, no suffering.

It was as if something tying us up had finally been undone, and the tears were washing it away.

"I feel like there are going to be a lot more tears from here on out, Minnalis."

"Yes, Master."

And then, we smiled.

The path we were on wasn't the right one, but it wasn't the wrong one, either.

So we beamed, with peace in our hearts, as the tears flowed.

The Monster's Blade of Hatching engulfed Slimo like a Venus flytrap, without the painful cry it had emitted when he emerged. After letting it eat the two halves of Zuily's head, I was done with it for now. Once it returned to the inside of the blade, I dispelled it.

"Minnalis!" I shouted just then.

"?!"

Suddenly, something came flying toward us. Eleven things, to be precise.

Dammit, will I make it?!

I had completely let down my guard, and my reactions were too slow. Switching into battle mode and ramping up my reaction time to max, I could see the flying things were spears, of simple make and specialized for throwing. They were tipped with a green liquid. Poison, no doubt. Four were headed toward me, and seven for Minnalis. I could see that she was trying to react as well, but she still had in her hands the rusty mallet she'd used to crush Dot's head, not her usual sword. With that weapon, she could only handle two of the spears, at most.

Casting my attention to the surrounding area, I detected sixteen goblins. The five who had not thrown their javelins seemed to be advancing on us at speed under cover of the projectiles.

But even though I could determine all of that in an instant, there was a big difference between realizing what was going on and addressing it. My reaction time was as sharp as it had ever been the last time around, but the ability of my body to keep up was still a long way off.

So the option to handle this cleanly and effortlessly was already off the table.

With this many goblins, I didn't have to worry about dragging things out. Without wasting a single drop of mana, I conjured in an instant the Soul Blade of Beginnings in my right hand and the Holy Sword of Retribution in my left. At the same time, I channeled as much mana as I could into my arms and legs, forcibly overriding the part of my body that sought to keep the flow in check for the sake of my limbs. In order to better understand the situation, I extended my magical senses into my surroundings.

Ignoring my aching muscles just for a second, I summoned up all the strength my current body could muster and leaped into the air. All of that took less than an instant. The inhuman speed with which I could make those kinds of decisions was precisely why I had earned the title "Master of Finesse" and had a Finesse score of SSS, the highest in the world.

I can let Minnalis handle the two in front. I just have to deal with the other nine.

By channeling mana into my legs and using Fleet-Foot, I could move even more quickly than my Agility score and Finesse allowed.

I ignored the four spears that had been aiming for me. Since they had all been on target, as soon as I left that spot, they posed no further threat.

That's four down.

It was only a short time, and I was controlling every ounce of my mana so that it wouldn't tear my body apart. Accelerating my creaking arm as fast as it would go, I swung the Holy Sword of Retribution at the frontmost of the three spears approaching Minnalis from her four o'clock position. Then with my other hand, I thrust the Soul Blade of Beginnings toward the one in the back, just scraping the spearhead and deflecting its trajectory. It flew toward the third spear and struck it like a billiard ball, knocking it off target as well. After seeing that, I killed my speed like my whole body was a shock absorber.

Just two left.

At that moment, the five monsters burst out of the thicket.

So these are Redcaps.

The Redcap was a member of the goblin family, but about a size smaller than the regular ones, and its head resembled a red hat, hence the name. They were a devious monster that excelled in group tactics. Apparently, the distinctive red markings on their heads were the blood of the prey they'd killed.

I quickly stepped off with one leg to change my body's direction, and regaining the speed I had just lost, rushed back over to Minnalis, where two of the Redcaps had appeared.

"Don't get carried away, you scum."

"Gaah…"

"Grah…"

I let my soul blades fall from my hands and reached out, grabbing both the Redcaps by their heads. Then I ran about a person's height into the air using Air Step, somersaulted, and with that momentum, tossed the goblins toward the last of the spears approaching Minnalis from her left. They crashed into them in mid-flight, whereupon the two Redcaps attacking us from that angle stopped in fright.

"Come on out, monsters!!"

There were still eleven Redcaps remaining in the bushes, the one still by me, one that had appeared behind Minnalis, and the two looking on in shock at the corpses of their allies I had just thrown into the spears.

I pulled back on the hilts of my two soul blades before they had time to fall and dashed over to the one attacking from the rear.

Rrgh! I can't keep my mana under control much longer!!

I was walking a tightrope, and my body was screaming at me to stop. Any more power and I'd be in danger. And it had still only been fifteen seconds.

If I'd had a little more MP left, I could have used my secret technique, but I had used most of it toying with Zuily's party.

I'm gonna feel sore tomorrow, that's for sure.

Right now, I was just barely managing to keep myself within limits, but I was missing a vital piece of my secret technique, and without it, my muscles were calling out in pain trying to emulate it.

Just as I was in a good mood at having some unexpected revenge fall into my lap, right at the end, these idiots had to spoil it.

I poured that resentment into my attack, slicing in the shape of a cross with my two blades, cutting the Redcap standing before me into quarters.

"Master!!"

"Minnalis, you take those two! I'll go after the ones still hiding!"

Once we got past the initial ambush, Minnalis could easily take on Redcaps in hand-to-hand combat, so I shot off into the forest without waiting for her reply. I sensed that the remaining goblins had not yet moved from their initial position and were still standing around about five meters away from us. Dispelling the Holy Sword of Retribution, I used my free hand to toss a couple of throwing knives at the two Redcaps on the right. The trees were obscuring a lethal strike, but that was no issue, for my knives were coated with a deadly poison of Minnalis's creation. They struck the two Redcaps, one in the arm, and one in the leg.

"Gyararargh?!"

"Gyururugh?!"

The poison got to work quickly, and I heard the creatures groan in agony. They were stupidly strong compared to regular goblins, though not as much as orcs, and so it would take them a little while to die, but they were goners now. I could ignore them.

I then turned to the one in front and hurled the Soul Blade of Beginnings at its heart, meanwhile conjuring up the very versatile Pyrachnid's Claw of Kindling in my right hand, and the Nephrite Blade of Verdure in my left. Once I heard the Redcap's death wail, I felt the Soul Blade of Beginnings return to its rightful place within me.

Weaving my way through the trees counterclockwise from where I'd started, I tore through the monster in one clean sweep. I sliced its throat, cleaved the flesh of its neck, stuck my fingers through its eye sockets, and hurled away its severed head, smashing it against a nearby tree.

After killing another one cleverly hiding in the bushes to ambush me, I swapped the Nephrite Blade of Verdure for the Soul Blade of Beginnings and skewered the two attempting to run away while I was distracted with their friend.

"Last one, huh?"

A final goblin charged at me in a suicidal rush.

"Gyaraaaargh!!"

"Shut up. I'll teach you to rain on my parade."

I sliced it in half, drawing the skirmish to a close at last.

"Oww... Man, I think I overdid it. Ahhh, so tired. So sleepy. Wanna go home. Wanna go to bed. Wanna just laze around and do nothing."

My body's demands issued forth from my lips as idle grumbles. I was still feeling good about what had happened with Zuily's party, but my body was going into full-on debt-collection mode. Even my reasoning was taking a back seat to the MP drunkenness. I'd taken a potion, but the effects would still take a while to clear.

"Now that I think about it, after I took care of the spears, I didn't have to keep trying so hard. Why didn't I realize that earlier?"

My arms and legs were going to be sore in the morning. I could already feel my joints creaking. That battle hadn't even been that long. *Is this all I can handle right now?* I thought with a sigh.

I was capable of much more than that. I knew I was.

"Ugh. Maybe I'll pick up some muscle rub from the apothecary when we get back. Nah, my MP will be recovered by then so I might as well just use the Nephrite Blade of Verdure... Damn, how did I ever survive without MP? I'll have to practice my Meditate skill a bit more... Ah."

Shit, I'm talking to myself again. I don't even notice when I'm doing it.

And right after Minnalis pointed it out the other day. I ruffled my hair.

Let's just take some trophies from the Redcaps and get back to... Urgh. I can't be bothered. Do I have to get them all? Bringing sixteen back to the guild is sure to cause a fuss, too...

Redcaps weren't much by themselves, but a group of sixteen was a force to be reckoned with, far beyond the capabilities of a newbie adventurer, as I ostensibly was.

Two or three would be far more manageable, at least that way I would *merely* be seen as an excellent novice with lots of training, rather than superhuman.

Yep, two or three will be fine. It's important not to stand out too much. Sure, the reward from the guild will be lost, but there are bigger things at stake. It's not just because I'm lazy, Minnalis.

I repeated my excuse to myself. Minnalis had been acting more and more like a bossy housewife with each passing day. What's that, you say? I could just hand the trophies in bit by bit so as not to attract attention? Well... I didn't think of that. Yeah, let's go with that.

And so I carved off the trophies of the nearest two to me and returned to Minnalis.

"Hmm?"

"..."

But when I got back to the clearing, there was a bizarre sight waiting for me.

"Hello? Ground control to Major Minnalis. Anyone home? ... What are you doing?"

The Redcap I'd sliced to pieces, the two I threw into the spears, and the two I let Minnalis shred to bits... For some reason, Minnalis seemed to have arranged the five monsters in a circle and was kneeling in the center. Her usually springy rabbit ears were drooping. I could almost see her dejection taking form behind her.

"I-I'm preparing for you to tell me off, Master. It's my job to keep an eye out for the enemy, and yet I was having so much fun taking out the trash that I didn't notice the monster attack..."

"Ahhh, don't worry about it, you can feel sorry for yourself when we get home. Right now, I just want to get back to the inn and enjoy a nice nap."

"Y-you're not going to scold me?"

"Why would I? I didn't notice them until the last second, either, so I don't really have the right. We've both got a lot to learn."

"You're...not going to dispose of me? You're going to let me stay as your slave? Stay as your partner in crime?"

"Huh? What's gotten into you? It wasn't your fault we got ambushed. Besides, if I could survive on my own, I wouldn't have taken a slave in the first place, and the Holy Sword of Retribution binds us together anyway. I couldn't leave you behind."

To be honest, she looked like she wanted to be punished, but I wasn't in the mood, so I pretended not to notice this. I could deal with that later.

"I guess the MP drunkenness hasn't worn off yet, because your thoughts are still in a weird place. Here, have another one."

"Hng! Ng...mnn...pahh..."

I forced another MP potion down her throat, and the blue liquid dripped from her lips. The teary look in her eyes was oddly suggestive. Usually, I'd be a little perturbed by a sight like this, but right now I was too tired to do anything about it. I just wanted to be under the covers again, and I wasn't about to fall asleep here. Whatever Minnalis had going on, it was going to have to wait until later, because I was heading back as soon as possible.

"Just get up. We're leaving."

"Ah... Yes, Master...," she said, rising to her feet and following my lead.

"For now, we'll head back to the guild and make our report as per the plan."

"I suppose so..."

"Hey, don't sound so depressed. Come on, stand up straight!"

"Ah... Oh! Yes, Master!"

I ruffled her long, black hair and set her mind to new thoughts.

"If you've got time to mope, think about revenge instead. We're only just getting started, Minnalis."

Perhaps it was because I was tired, or perhaps it was because of the MP drunkenness, but I couldn't hide what I was feeling. A broad smile spread across my face.

"Ohhh, just imagining it gives me the shivers. Killing those guys made me feel a little better, but it's not enough. Nowhere near."

"..."

My eyes narrowed, and my lips curled upward.

"I just get so excited thinking about my revenge inching closer and closer to completion. Feel sorry for yourself if you wish, Minnalis, but you're missing out on all the fun. Our next goal is just beyond these trees, remember."

"...and that's about it."

We were back in town, giving our report to the guild. Hansel had gone to relieve himself in the bushes when he was attacked by Redcaps. We were alerted by his screams and managed to kill the two that came for us, but fearing for our lives, we ran back to town, leaving him behind.

"We heard a terrible scream from Hansel, the noble boy, just a little before we finished fighting, so I think he..."

"I see... I'm sorry for the boy, but I think you two did the right thing. Redcaps specialize in group and ambush tactics, so I think if you'd gone to help him, it would have only ended even worse."

Of course, we didn't mention Zuily's party at all.

Incidentally, it was a different person at the reception desk this time, one of the burly men. He was older and more experienced, and he understood the situation clearly.

"But I can't believe Redcaps have spread to that part of the forest...," he muttered.

"Indeed. Here are the trophies as proof," I said, placing the two monster remains on the counter along with all the goblin ears we collected. The receptionist man took them carefully and eyed them with a serious look.

"Yep, this is a Redcap scalp, no doubt about it. Normally, they live in the hills deeper into the woods, but occasionally a stray pack of about half a dozen or so will wander into the lower reaches. All we can say is you guys got unlucky."

"I guess so."

Hmm? That was quite a large group we ran into, then.

Although we were downplaying their number to avoid suspicion, we had actually run into sixteen of the creatures. That didn't feel like some stray pack...did they *all* get lost? Or was there something more to it?

Now that I think about it, before the undead army attacked, there were reports of heightened monster assaults. Could this be the precursor to that?

The first time I had come to Elmia, a swarm of undead had suddenly attacked out of nowhere. It turned out after the villagers were possessed by demons and the soldiers put them to death, the evil mana leaked out of their bodies and possessed the corpses of monsters. Those monsters then rose up and started killing other monsters to increase their ranks, before finally assaulting the City of Learning itself.

I had once stayed in the ruins of that village after the world turned against me. It was a cursed place. Deep scars in the earth still held vestiges of dark magics, and flowers bearing purple and yellow petals covered the rubble.

Last time, it was that piece of shit spellcaster Eumis who shared with us her knowledge of the undead, and it was an A-rank party comprising me, that damn princess, and the shithead knight commander who fought them off... I wonder what'll happen this time?

It would still be another two months or so before that attack would happen. First, there would be an attack formed of goblins, Redcaps, and boars from the mountains. Luckily, there happened to be another A-rank party in the area, and coupled with the soldiers from Elmia, the city repelled that attack. That would happen about ten days prior. After fending them off, the city would send an investigation team into the forest to determine its cause, and that meant they were just barely able to respond to the army of undead in time. However...

That forest was the same one stretching between this town and the city of Elmia, so it wouldn't be strange for its influences to be felt here, as well. It was likely that Redcaps appearing where they normally didn't was another sign of that development in the works.

While I was thinking about all this, the receptionist finished counting my trophies and produced a sack of coins.

"There's no request for Redcaps, so we'll pay the normal fee. As for the goblins, here's the reward for those."

He tipped out a few coins onto the countertop and put the sack away.

"And I'd say we're already looking at about E-rank levels of skill for coming back unharmed after fighting Redcaps, even if it was only two. Keep completing your requests and we might see fit to increase your rank."

"I see, thank you."

"And just a little word of advice, if I may. Zuily's party may be D rank, but I haven't heard good things about them at all. I think it'd be better for you if you try to steer clear of them. I heard about your wager, and I'll pass the results on to them when they show up. You two kids head home for now, and let me handle them."

"That's very nice of you, thank you very much."

This guy's ripped, handsome, *and* nice. Not fair.

I bowed to the gruff-yet-polite receptionist, and then Minnalis and I left the guild.

CHAPTER 4
Emerald Nightmare

Ⅰf you lived your life until the very end, blissfully unaware you were being deceived until the moment you died, would that not be a happy existence?

It sounds lovely to me. A fairy-tale ending. Because dead people know not what the future brings.

So... So?

Is that really what I want?

Because I feel content, even though I can't have that anymore. I'm glad I know I was betrayed. Even if it means I had to fall through the cracks in the earth and drink of the black mires of hell.

...Ahhh, I suppose there's simply no rhyme or reason to it. It's just the way it is.

To be human or monster. To be sane or insane.
Even now, the fragments of my broken heart still urge me on.

*　　*　　*

My happiness was lost, my life was unfair, my dignity was robbed, and I was thrust into the pits of despair.

But I still have time. Time to laugh at the world, holding my mishmash of a heart in my hands.

...Even if that is the path of evil.

It was ten days after we exacted revenge upon Zuily's party. In the first week, we stopped at Golet, and as usual, we spent the time sitting around, eating Minnalis's cooking, discussing torture methods, and honing our skill proficiencies.

I was worried we might arouse suspicion leaving town immediately after Zuily's party failed to show up. The guild shared information between its branches using magic items, so in order to appear natural, I had dropped in on the guild as normal and informed them I was leaving for Elmia.

Now we were in the large forest that stretched between our target city and the town of Golet. The distance between the two locations was not far, and we were already past the halfway point. We were camped only a day or two from our destination when it happened.

"Master, wake up."

"Hmrh...? Are we being attacked?"

My eyes shot open, and adrenaline surged through my body when I heard her words. It was a little before dawn, and the sky was just starting to brighten. It would not be long before the sun made its first appearance on the horizon.

"I don't think so, but I can hear the sounds of combat not far from here. They might make their way here soon; we should at least hide."

She must have been channeling magic into her ears to use the "Enhanced Hearing" skill. Her rabbit ears were pricked up and twitching. As a human, I wasn't able to learn Enhanced Hearing, but I could still make out the faint sound of metal clashing against metal far off in the distance.

"It's coming from farther up the road." I sighed. "Usually we'd just be able to ignore it."

I wanted to avoid getting involved in unrelated quarrels and stirring up the wrath of God as much as possible, but unfortunately, this time I couldn't. It wasn't clear how far away the fighting was, but it was undoubtably in front of us, toward the city of Elmia. In order to determine whether we should ignore it or intervene, first we would have to see what the situation was. I'd already learned the hard way that going in without enough information could be fatal.

"Let's go."

"Yes, Master."

Packing up the campsite into our sack as quickly as we could, we made our way carefully toward the source of the sound, with me getting ready to draw my soul blades at any moment. Minnalis, too, placed her hand on the sword at her belt and recast her illusion.

Incidentally, she was on her eighth sword of the mass-produced ones we had bought at the capital. The seventh had taken us through the dungeon, but it only lasted a few more monsters after that before it needed to be laid to rest.

"...Adventurers and...bandits, I think?"

It appeared to be a fight between two groups of people. A bunch of shabbily dressed men were surrounding a horse and carriage. Defending it was a group of adventurers.

Adventurers on an escort mission being ambushed by bandits. Not much else to say about it, really.

"Hmm, looks like the hired hands are going to lose."

They were holding out well so far against a force twice their size, but it was clear their luck would soon run out.

"That settles it," I announced.

"Indeed, Master."

We nodded at each other and disappeared into the right-hand side of the forest before being spotted. We could have just as easily walked straight through, but who knew what that might lead to? As for stepping in and supporting either side, well, that was entirely out of the question. I couldn't care less if the adventurers or the bandits won. I would gain nothing by helping either of them. So we circled around through the forest, forging a path through the gaps in the trees. I was still feeling a little irritated that my sleep had been disturbed.

Then something happened that made me wish I'd gone left instead.

"*Brooouuuuaaaaahhhhh!*"

"J-just my luck…!"

"Well, if we were lucky, we wouldn't be here, Master."

What appeared was a monster resembling a large, bipedal pig. Orcs were far taller than their goblin brethren, standing about as tall as a human, but with physical strength far superior to any man.

However, this one was clearly not your everyday orc, for it was almost twice that height, with dark reddish-black skin that could shrug off all but the hardiest physical blows.

…It was a variant orc known as a Black Orc, or Big Orc, to give its common name.

"*Bruuuooah!*"

Black Orc
Lv54

Male • Monster

HP: 534/2172 (1974)   MP: 121/221

Strength: 801   Stamina: 424

Vitality: 1712 (1465)   Agility: 314

Magic: 41   Resistance: 33

Intrinsic Abilities: Blackhide
Skills: Enhance Life Lv 2, Harden Lv 2,
Intimidate Lv 2, Resist Status Lv 4,
Food Recovery Lv 3, Omnivore Lv 3
Status: Bleeding

"I don't suppose there's any chance it's just a regular orc that just so happens to be big and black?"

"This is no time for jokes, Master!"

Even if there was a 1 percent chance my wishful thinking could come true, reality came back at me with a big, fat *no*.

"*Brooooooaaaaahhh!!*"

"Leave it to me!"

The Black Orc swung its right fist at us as if we were little more than shrubs in its way. I heard the whoosh of air and the splintering of wood as it struck a nearby tree.

"Damn, we can't fight it here. Let's get back to the road!"

Just like with that goblin with the cursed sword, taking a solid hit here would be pretty bad. Minnalis could probably tank a couple hits if she defended them perfectly, but her sword couldn't. I, on the other hand, would be toast. The orc's Agility was low, and it was rather dumb, so it would be easy enough to dodge its attacks, but the trees here would get in the way. They didn't bother the Black Orc so much because it could just mow them down with its attacks. I couldn't ignore them outright like it could. Therefore, it was wiser to fall back to the open space of the road where we could move around more easily.

"It looks like the fight there is still ongoing, Master! Let's lead it there, and perhaps we can use them as a decoy— Hrh!"

"*Brrrrraaaaghhh!*"

This time the Black Orc swung its left arm down, like a lightning bolt from the sky. Minnalis jumped aside to evade it.

"Goddammit, calm down!!!"

I tossed a throwing knife at the Black Orc's eyes, but it turned its face aside and was struck only on the cheek.

"*Bruugh!*"

"Damn, not even enough to leave a mark..."

The knife had been coated in Minnalis's poison, but it didn't even have the slightest effect. Still, I threw several more knives as a distraction before conjuring up the Challenger's Blade of Adversity. Watching the Black Orc brush aside the knives like they were a mere nuisance, we leaped out of the forest and into the road.

"Wha—?! That's a Black Orc!"

"Eek! What's it doin' here?!"

I didn't know if that was the adventurers or the bandits, but they echoed my sentiments perfectly.

The Black Orc seemed pleased to find even more prey and made a cheerful-sounding grunt. I gripped the Challenger's Blade of Adversity in both hands and faced it. This weapon was shaped like a pair of tonfa from our world, except that the striking part was replaced with a gleaming blade that curved gently inward, like a sickle, with the edge on the outside. The handle was located about two-thirds of the way down the one-meter-long blade on the blunt side. The two blades were bright red with accents of blue and black, and even now they seemed hungry to slice into their prey.

"Brrrrrgh!!"

The Black Orc struck the man standing in shock before it with its enormous arm, then he fell to the ground, unmoving, as if every single bone in his body had been crushed. Judging by his dress, he was probably one of the bandits. They should have fled as soon as they heard the Black Orc's cry, but I guess they couldn't bear to retreat just when they were on the verge of winning.

"Oink, oink, oink!!"

The Black Orc picked up the man's corpse and dropped it in its mouth, gobbling up the whole thing in a matter of seconds.

"R-run awa… G-gyah!"

I grabbed a bandit who happened to come within reach, channeled my mana into my arm, and hurled him at the Black Orc's right shoulder.

"Bruaaaagh!"

"Eeeek!!"

The Black Orc, of course, met the human cannonball with its fist in midair. The bandit's bones splintered, and he died without even having the chance to scream. Grateful for the distraction, I slipped in beneath the Black Orc's blind spot and swung my blade at its shins, sinking it halfway into its flesh.

"Bruaaaaargh!"

"Dammit, just how resistant to physical attacks can you be?"

I had meant to slice clean through, but the attack only left the creature lightly wounded. Still, it caused it to leap back, seemingly wary of me.

The Black Orc was, of course, a type of orc. The guild assigned it a rank of D+, meaning that a party of five D-rank adventurers, or two C-rank adventurers, was needed to slay it. Usually, the highest rank an adventurer was expected to obtain was B, and they were considered fully fledged at D, so that should give you an idea of just how strong this thing was.

Incidentally, the royal knight commander's squadron was still only a five-man-band at this point, probably around C, and the guards I fought when I'd escaped were about E+ at best.

The Black Orc's power surpassed all other orcs, but its true strength lay in its intrinsic ability, Blackhide, that gave it unparalleled physical defenses. Any ordinary weapon would not only fail to leave a scratch but would also very likely be damaged in the process. However, it was exceedingly weak to magic attacks, and this led to a lower rank than it would otherwise deserve. However...

"Damn, I picked the wrong soul blade."

Right now, we had no way of performing magic attacks. Minnalis could create poisons with mana, but poison magic couldn't do any direct damage by itself. Those poisons still had to be applied physically, and in addition to that, the Black Orc was resistant to all forms of status ailments. Even if we tried creating a toxic cloud to have it inhale the poison, that could likely backfire on us.

I had already seen from watching the fight that there were no magic-users among either the adventurers or the bandits. Since our attacks were having little effect, perhaps it would be easier to take advantage of its low Agility and simply make a break for it, but...

"Master, what's the matter?"

"It's already been weakened. It seems like a shame."

I didn't know how it had happened, but the Black Orc had already taken quite a bit of damage. In the light of the dawn, I could see cuts and blood all over its body.

"Damn, why'd it have to show up here? Retreat!"

That was the voice of the bandit leader, taking several of his men and falling back into the forest on the opposite side of where the Black Orc had appeared.

"Come on, client, forget the cart and run!!"

"B-but wait, my precious merchandise is still inside...!!"

"You wanna stick around and wind up in the ground?! Get moving already!!"

This time it was the leader of the adventurers, who huddled around the client and took off down the road.

"Get outta here, you two!! You've only got swords! Nothin' but magic is gonna finish that creature off!" the leader shouted, before fleeing alongside their companions without waiting to see how things turned out. It was a quick and rational decision. I guessed this person must have been a veteran, used to putting themselves in harm's way.

"But I hate to see all this experience go to waste. We can duke it out a lot more easily now that the peanut gallery is gone, too."

I checked his status again, and the Black Orc's HP had gone down from 534 to 498. Its bleeding appeared to be draining its health, as well.

"I think we should leave it and retr—"

"Minnalis, did you know that Black Orc flesh is an important research component, the price of which is measured in gold?"

"Master, I think we should stay and defeat it! Money is the solution to many of life's problems!"

"…We have plenty of cash already thanks to your penny-pinching."

"That doesn't matter! You can never have too much!"

"That's true."

I felt like it was more her miserliness than her keen economic senses doing the talking, but I kept that to myself.

"*Bruuuooooaaaaghhh!*" The orc, tired of keeping its distance, charged in, swinging its fists.

"Minnalis, cover me. Look out for its insane strength and its resistance to physical attacks and status conditions."

"Okay, Master."

As the Black Orc swung its fist, I took my stance with the tonfa. Dashing between the creature's legs, I delivered another stroke to exactly the same place I had inflicted the previous wound.

"*Braaaaagh! Rraagh!*"

The Black Orc gave a squeal of pain and swung around, launching another fist, but I rolled to avoid it. As it turned to pursue me, one of Minnalis's poisoned knives flew toward its eyes. Just like with mine, it dodged it by moving its head, but…

"It may be big, but it's still as dumb as any orc."

"*Bruuoooaaaagh!!*"

Minnalis's second knife sliced open the sack tied to the first.

Inside was an irritant poison. While it didn't do any damage, it scattered into the Black Orc's eyes, causing it to collapse in pain. It didn't count as a status condition either, so its Resist Status Lv 4 did nothing. Clutching its eye with one hand, it swung at me with the other. Its fist plowed through the adventurers' cart, reducing it to woodchips in an instant.

"You're never gonna hit me swinging wildly!"

In order to dodge the randomly flailing arm, I moved over to the orc's other side where it couldn't reach me. I had only been aiming at its legs so far, but now I could aim at its top half as well. I moved over to its flank and drove both the tips of the Challenger's Blade of Adversity into a wound on its side before driving them apart. The Orc's red flesh spilled out from beneath its black skin.

"Braaaaaghhh?!"

"Minnalis!!"

"Yes, Master!!" She tossed me a poison-coated knife, and I jammed it into the open wound.

"Brrruuuaaaaaaaaarrrrgggghhhh!!"

The Black Orc gave a loud cry of pain and pulled the knife from its side.

"You said its status resistance was high, but I didn't expect it to be this tolerant. I was quite proud of that paralysis poison, too…," muttered Minnalis.

"No, I think it is affecting it, just a little bit."

The Black Orc's movements were noticeably slower after removing the knife. Checking its status, I saw that it now had another condition of "Paralyzed (S)." Its HP had decreased to 200, as well.

"All right, time to finish it off…"

"Witness the terrible shout of the wind spirits! *Lightning!!*"

A peal of thunder interrupted my thoughts. Right where I was about to step, a bolt of green lightning split the air in two.

"Brooaaaaaghhh!"

"Wha—?!"

The sudden spell caught me off guard. The wind spell finished off the Black Orc's remaining HP in an instant, and it ended its life with a final wail of pain.

"This spell…is that woman's…"

"Master, look over there, and prepare to conceal your *emotions*."

At Minnalis's words, I knew my guess had been correct. She'd already activated her Iron Mask skill.

"Are you two all right? I came to help!"

I slowly turned my head and looked down the road ahead of us. Although I knew what was coming, I hadn't had enough time to mentally prepare, so for a split second, the shock was visible on my face.

"Ahhh, I never expected to see *you* before I got to Elmia," I muttered, fighting back the grin trying to show itself on my face.

At last, number one.

I've come back from death to see you again…

…Eumis Elmia the Spellcaster.

Where should I begin? There's so much I want to say to you. So much I want to *do* to you.

But one thing is certain.

I want to see you sink deep into eternal torment, where darkness reigns supreme.

Try as I might, I just couldn't stop the corners of my lips curling upward into a smirk.

"I'm so sorry. I heard there was a Black Orc and hurried over as fast as I could… I didn't realize you'd nearly defeated it already."

There, ducking her head apologetically while she spoke in a slow, gentle tone, was a young woman clad in a well-tailored mage robe, holding a wooden staff clearly rich in mana. Her hair was a dark

green, yet somehow bright, like fresh leaves. On the right side of her head was a wooden hairpin shaped like a flower, and on the other side, a long tuft of hair fell past her shoulder. Her hair glimmered in the half-risen sun, beautiful and fleeting.

Eumis Elmia.

As evidenced by her name, she was the daughter of the lord of the city of Elmia. She was an aristocrat, a magical researcher, and a proficient user in her own right. She had been a valuable member of the team on our quest to vanquish the demon lord.

"I just thought you might have trouble against the Black Orc because you two are sword-users and not mages...," she said. "Oh, I'm simply making excuses. It's my fault for not making sure I understood the situation."

"Ah, no worries," I replied. "There were some aspects of the situation that were out of our control, too."

What I wanted to shout was, *"You're damn right! How dare you snatch our kill, you piece of shit!"* but I resisted and swallowed my anger behind a fake smile.

It wasn't the time for revenge yet. Unlike with the princess, I knew exactly what was going on here. There was no need to rush.

"Pardon me for asking," she began, "but how on earth did you do all this to a Black Orc without magic? I mean..."

Minnalis and I were dressed in the beginner adventurers' gear we'd bought in the capital, covered in black robes. I'd bought them because I thought we might stand out otherwise; two lone adventurers traveling together without even hiring a carriage, dressed in clothes the townsfolk might wear. However, it was obvious at a glance that they were nothing impressive. Certainly not capable of allowing us to fell the Black Orc.

"Ahhh, well..."

"Is it perhaps something to do with that strange sword you

wield?" she asked. "Oh, where are my manners? It isn't proper to ask an adventurer about their abilities."

"Oh no, it may look strange, but this is just a normal sword. The Black Orc had already been weakened when we encountered it. We were finding it hard to deal any damage, so we were hoping to tire it out."

"Oh, I see... I do not know who would chase a Black Orc all the way here. Seeing as its attacker is no longer around, perhaps the monster got the better of them...?"

Eumis made a thinking gesture, a slightly sad expression on her face, before shaking her head.

"In any case, it doesn't change the fact that I stole your target. I'll let you have all its materials. In fact, I have a favor to ask... Could you let me have the monster's body?"

"You want its body?"

"Yes, I'll pay you for it. How does five gold pieces sound? I have a class 2 magic bag, too, so I'll take care of transporting it."

Magic bags were specially designed for holding magic items. Depending on their strength, they were given a ranking. The very best were special class, below that were first class, and it went all the way to class 10. A class 2 magic bag had a capacity about the size of a studio apartment and could be shrunk down to a twentieth that size.

No magic bag could hold an unlimited number of items like the Squirrel's Blade of Holding could, but in return, they didn't use MP. Unlike the Squirrel's Blade, though, the magic could only reduce the weight and size instead of eliminating it entirely. This meant it would still get heavier the more items you put in it. The opening grew to allow you to put large items inside, but cramming them in was still pretty inconvenient, since unlike our bag, it wouldn't automatically suck the items in once it got near them.

Furthermore, the more random stuff you accumulated, the

harder it was to pick out the one you needed when you wanted it. And finally, of course, they could get quite expensive if you wanted a high-class one.

Most veteran adventurers carried them around, but the best an intermediate adventurer could hope to buy if they wanted to splurge for something that would last them their whole life was a class 5 bag.

With my riches, I could have easily picked up a class 4 bag for Minnalis and me while we were in the capital, but even taking the 5 percent MP cap reduction into account, our method of storage was clearly superior. I could grab throwing knives simply by sticking my hand in the opening and wishing for them, without having to waste precious time rummaging around inside; no matter how much I put in it, its weight never changed; and there was no limit on the number of things I could store. I didn't feel the need to spend upward of ten gold pieces on a magic bag that was inferior in almost every way.

"Wow, a class 2 magic bag. That's impressive. Oh, and don't worry about the price at all. It just kind of fell into our laps, and we don't have any way of transporting it ourselves. I have no idea what a Black Orc is worth, either. I'm just happy to sell it to a pretty lady like you," I joked, in a way that, even if it was obviously an act, didn't seem unnatural. However, I immediately regretted it.

Even if I didn't mean them, those words of flattery tasted like rotten fruit in my mouth, a concoction of bitterness and acidity that made me want to throw up. I was suddenly gripped by an overwhelming urge to smash my face into that of the Black Orc before my expression faltered, but that would definitely give cause for alarm, so I refrained.

"Tee-hee, it's a little above market price that I'm offering. You may confirm later in town if you so wish."

If she were really trying to scam us, she would at least show a hint of emotion while doing it, but as always, she showed not the slightest amount of interest in other people.

"You may call me Eumis. Perhaps our paths shall cross again, should you call upon the Halls of Learning at Elmia."

"Perhaps they shall."

"Well, then. I shall now take my leave. I was on my way to collect pipewort. Assemble forthwith: *Create Golem.*"

Eumis cast her incantation, whereupon sand, rocks, and boulders rose out of the ground and took form, resulting in two tough-looking stone figures. Eumis handed them the bag, and they started loading the still-smoking carcass of the Black Orc inside.

"One, two... Here you go: five gold pieces."

Eumis counted out five coins and placed them in my hand. Then she bowed, and set off down the road, leaving the golems to finish their work. We headed in the opposite direction, toward the city. Once she was out of sight, Minnalis relaxed her Iron Mask skill.

"Well, that was a surprise," she said. "I didn't think we'd be meeting her so soon."

"Yeah. I really wasn't prepared for that," I replied.

"Perhaps you should have been practicing Iron Mask. I don't think she realized anything, but I didn't like the shade your face turned when you flattered that woman... Like when you called her pretty."

I didn't quite catch what Minnalis muttered at the end, but seeing the unpleasant expression on her face, I thought it wise not to make her repeat herself.

"I don't need that skill. It'll only make us *more* suspicious if both of us are completely stone-faced whenever we meet anyone new. I may not be able to find it in myself to be overly cordial, but about this level, I can handle."

"If you say so, Master. If that's the case, shall I try to force a grin next time as well? It might well ruin my entire day, though."

"Join the club. Maybe we can go out somewhere as a reward. Or we could just both go to bed and sulk if you prefer."

"Both go to bed and sulk...? That sounds quite nice, actually."

"Oh? You into that sort of thing, Minnalis?"

I had thought her quite the productive type. She didn't seem like one for lazing around in bed doing nothing.

"Well... I mean...if that's what you want to do, Master..."

"Hmm? Whatever, let's go for the first option today. We'll treat ourselves to a nice inn in town. That's not too strange considering we've just been on a long journey, and we can go out for food instead of making you cook."

"Actually, I'd prefer to prepare our meal myself. It helps me clear my mind."

"Mmm...but I'm always making you do that, Minnalis. I think you should take a break. We can probably borrow a kitchen, but I think we might as well let others handle the grub while we're in town."

"It's okay; I love to cook. Besides, I don't like my cooking to be compared to that of others. Or are you saying you're not satisfied with the food I make?"

"...Minnalis, you can be very cunning sometimes."

"Oh, were you not aware, Master? Women are made of such tricks." She smiled, exuding a little of the erotic charm she usually only displayed while drunk.

"Well, there's a fine line between being cunning and being dishonest," I said. "Make sure it doesn't get to your head. You don't want to turn into someone like that."

Minnalis's face fell, and her eyes smoldered with black, hate-filled flames. She was thinking about Lucia, one of her sworn enemies. I had seen her myself when the Holy Sword of Retribution had forced me to view her memories.

"Well, in any case, no. I'm very satisfied with your food, Minnalis. It's delicious."

"Ah...when you say it like that, it's a little embarrassing," she replied, her face suddenly losing all emotion.

"Do you really have to use your Iron Mask skill?" I asked. "Look, it's just, I don't know, maybe you could learn something. I just think it's worth eating out once in a while when all you do is cook all the time."

"I...suppose that's true. I *have* been finding my repertoire somewhat lacking as of late. If I steal all the things you like, then *I* can be the one to make them from now on."

"R-right, yeah. That sounds...good?"

I seemed to have stoked the fires of her culinary heart rather more than I'd anticipated. As we continued on toward Elmia, I swore I felt something unfathomable lurking behind that expressionless mask of hers.

Then I realized something.

"You know, we haven't even eaten yet."

"So we haven't. I'm also feeling a little worn out from that fight. How about we stop for breakfast?"

Minnalis's breakfast that morning was rather more extravagant than usual, and we broke out the expensive eggs.

"Haah...haah...haah..."

I ran through the dark forest, between thick trunks and through overgrown bushes. My HP was fine, but getting out of that trap had cost me nearly all of my MP.

"Grh!!"

I felt a powerful spell. My magical detection field alerted me to the incoming attack, and I launched myself sideways. Not a second later, a green lightning bolt struck the ground where I had stood. There was a loud, dull sound, like something heavy being dropped from a very high place, and the poor tree the lightning struck exploded into blackened wooden shards.

Such power. It had to be her. It was restrained so that given my current Resistance stat, it wouldn't kill me, but instead leave me immobile and barely alive. She always was the best at tuning her spells.

"Dammit!!"

With my MP as low as it was, there was no way I could activate the perfect defense of the Aegis Blade of Shielding. There were still spells I could cast, but not while I was running around trying to dodge.

"There's only one thing for it..."

Just as I made up my mind, I entered a healthy-looking clearing. I paused to get my soul blades in order.

"Oh dear, are we already finished playing tag?" came a voice.

"Eumis..."

There she was, Eumis Elmia. Wearing the same gentle smile and the same green robe. My old friend. And now, my enemy.

"Surrender now, and I will make your death painless. We've always gotten on well, and unlike the princess, I harbor no particular disdain for you. Don't worry, I'm quite adept at ending a specimen's life without causing harm."

Her usual smile was now devoid of all traces of the affection it had once held. An innocent light, almost like madness, filled her eyes. It was plain to see she wouldn't feel a shred of guilt over killing me.

A battle was unavoidable. Somewhere in my heart, I hoped we

might still be able to talk things out, but the look in her eyes crushed those dreams. She wasn't staring at a person. To her, I was merely a thing, materials to be harvested.

"Why?! Why are you trying to kill me?!"

It was hardly worth asking the question. I already knew she didn't see me as human. They were empty words I just had to ask. Even now, I still didn't want to believe it.

"Why? I've already told you, many times. You are possessed of great power, enough now to defeat a Dungeon Guardian by yourself, and even hold your own against the demon lord. With you as an ingredient, I could create the ultimate magic item, my life's crowning work! At last, my name will be engraved into the statue at Elmia... No, the honor bestowed upon me will be even greater! This will take my fame within Elmia to new heights!"

Her eyes were wide and starry.

"But you're already famous! Why do you need more notoriety?"

"It's not enough. From traveling with you, I've developed a reputation as a spellcaster, that's true. But only artificers who create powerful magical items have their names carved on the monument. It's been my dream since I was a little girl, but I cannot do it as I am now."

Eumis looked dejected, before she suddenly perked up with hope and looked at me.

"That's why you have to let me kill you! Oh, I'm looking forward to it so much!"

Her eyes glittered. Her long-held dream was finally within reach. That I had to die to achieve it didn't weigh on her mind at all.

"You...you would betray me for *that*?!"

"It may not seem like much to you, but I could wish for nothing greater. It's like how, to us, the demon lord was a blight upon the land, but to you, she wasn't. See?"

She adopted the tone one might use when dealing with an

uncooperative child. There was no doubt in her mind that her actions were justified. She went on, spewing words that sounded plain evil.

"It's all over for you, anyway. The kingdom is no longer your ally, and so any hope of returning to your world is gone. Why don't you just give up?"

"Shut up, I'll find a way back, if it's the last thing I do."

"You sure are a stubborn man. There is no such way."

She smiled another innocent smile, tinged with venom.

"Your dream is *broken*. There is nothing left for you but to become the ingredient to mine."

"Rgh…! Eumiiiiiis!!"

I could bear it no longer. Whatever part of me still hoped we could be friends shattered. There was no more room for negotiation. I couldn't even allow her to go on living. She was my enemy, pure and simple. Somehow, I always knew it would end like this.

"Wind Slice: Cross Slash!"

I drew the Weasel's Blade of Wind, a green katana streaked with red, and delivered a pair of cross-shaped slices. Invisible blades of wind rushed toward Eumis, but it was child's play for her to avoid such an obvious attack.

"Phlogiston Blast!"

Eumis cast her spell without even reciting the full chant, and a tremendous explosion obliterated those blades before they even got close. Her spell used water magic to generate water, wind magic to electrolyze it into hydrogen and oxygen, and fire magic to detonate it. It was I who taught her the theory, and we had worked on the spell together. Clouds of dust filled my vision. I knew Eumis would rely on a method like this to consume the least amount of mana possible.

"Darkness, take form: *Illusory Figure!*"

Speaking the magic words, I drew my other soul blade, the Husk Blade of Shadows. Five figures who looked exactly like me leaped out of the dust, cloaked in mana. They were so perfect, even Eumis couldn't tell them apart at a glance.

"Gr... *Pincushion!!*"

Three of the figures rushed toward Eumis, who unleashed a cone-shaped blast of tiny stone spears. One near the back managed to block the spears with his sword, but the other two were not so lucky. One was skewered through the chest, the other in the elbow, before both reverted to shadows and disappeared.

"So they disappear when I hit anywhere except the sword? You must really be running out of MP if these are the best illusions you can produce."

Eumis fired another lightning bolt, and a searing green light burned my eyes. I jumped aside, but she was aiming for the tree behind me. I was unable to avoid the explosion of wooden shards, and my final clone vanished, leaving only the true form standing some distance away.

"*Lava Prison.*"

"Grh!!"

A magic circle appeared around me, and magma burst up out of the ground, surrounding me in a cage-like lattice of stone.

"Now, the game of hide-and-seek is over."

"...Yeah, it is."

"That cage will burn you to death. I wouldn't want you to sustain too much damage, so could you hold still while I finish you off? It'll be a far more pleasant death than the alternative." She grinned. Now I had no choice but to accept it. This was Eumis's true nature. She didn't change after we defeated Leticia. She was always like this, deep down. Why hadn't I realized it sooner? I had spent over two years by her side.

And it wasn't just her. The princess and all my other party members were the same. Why did I never get to know them? Every day since I killed Leticia, I asked myself the same questions.

How had I missed it?

If only I had noticed earlier.

How many times had those thoughts run through my mind? Too many to count.

"Any last words? I can grant you a final request," offered Eumis. I was standing solemn, silent, and still, the face of resignation.

"There's nothing more I have to say to the likes of you," I replied. "But... There is one thing... I suppose I have to apologize to her one more time. After all she's done for me, here she is saving me again."

"What are— Wh-what?! What's that light?! *Lightn*—"

"See you, psycho."

With those parting words, I activated my teleportation stone and disappeared without a trace.

The location I teleported to was beyond a vast mountain range. The rain was pouring, soaking my clothes and chilling my body. With no time to waste, I found a nearby cave and, after checking it was free of monsters, dispelled the illusions I had cast on myself.

"Ugh, oh god..."

I looked down at myself. The illusions had done a good job of hiding the damage. Deep wounds covered my body, and my equipment was smeared with blood. There were gashes all across my skin, and in some places, the cuts had bitten deeply into the flesh.

"It's a good thing I didn't call her an idiot, because if *she's* an idiot then I don't want to know what that makes me..." A wry smile crossed my lips.

It was thought that once you ran out of MP, you could no longer cast magic, but that wasn't quite true. If you could withstand the massive pain that ensued, it could certainly be done.

The price had to be paid somehow. If you had no MP, then the cost came out of your HP instead, and consequently you incurred intense pain and grievous injuries.

"I was a prodigy, you know. As a child, the power of my magic was beyond compare, but I always used too much MP and ended up hurting myself."

"Ha-ha-ha, yeah, I can see that. You're such a scatterbrain, Leticia."

"Hrm...? Why do you find that so funny, Kaito?"

"Even after she's gone, I'm still racking up debts with her."

If we had never played that game of cards, wagering embarrassing stories from our childhoods, I might not have been able to escape this time.

I took an HP and MP potion from my pack. I sprinkled the HP potion over my wounds, while the MP potion I downed in a single gulp. With the small amount of MP the potion restored, I used my soul blade to light a fire with some fuel stones from my pack. They were smokeless and burned longer than wood. As I sat by the fire, I sought to escape my weary thoughts.

"I wonder how many times I have to apologize for calling her a scatterbrain."

I imagined her sulking face, and a gentle smile rose to my lips.

"...I wish I could see you again. It's rough being alone, Leticia."

There was a time I thought my dreams could come true. That I'd return to my world with Leticia by my side. My family would be so surprised. I didn't know what they thought of me now, but I knew they would lose their shit when they saw her. How would Mai react when she heard I'd gotten into a relationship? We'd always been such close siblings; if I suddenly disappeared and returned with a girlfriend, I bet she wouldn't speak to me for months.

Suehiko and Kenta would weep bitter tears at the sight of me with such a pretty girl. Yuuto was always flirting with his girlfriend, so he wouldn't. Those two lovebirds were definitely still together, and he'd probably congratulate me for ending up like him.

It would be a lot of work, for sure. But with Leticia and her beautiful smile, anything was possible.

If only this were the dream, and the dream were reality instead. Just as Eumis said, it was all impossible now.

As I surrounded myself in those feeble thoughts, the sky outside gradually darkened, and as my eyes closed, I realized I was dreaming of my old memories again, and soon I would wake.

"Good morning, Master, it's time to get up."

"...Urgh... Five more minutes, please...," I moaned, the exact same thing I had said in the town of Golet.

I had just had the worst dream ever. It must have been because I ran into her yesterday. I demanded a redo.

It was only the second time around that I learned the importance of beds. Duvets stuffed with the warmest monster down, pillows of magical cotton, sheets woven from the magic silkworm's silk, and mattresses made from a fantastical plant known as the springytree.

I never knew happiness could be found in nothing more than a comfortable sleep. I had always been vigilant, and never rested in inns when I could avoid it. My bedding was always the hard roots of trees, my pillow the cold ground, with little more than a filthy rag for cover. My magical barrier was always alerting me to intruders, too, and I could never enjoy a proper, deep sleep. Of course, we still keep our guards up while sleeping, but at least we have comfy beds, and the threat I face isn't anywhere near as dangerous as it was before.

The beds in Golet were a lucky find, but these ones were a level above. Which was why I was so annoyed such a terrible dream had to spoil my first night in them.

"Please, just a little more…"

"No, Master. Get up, unless you want me to tear away your blanket again."

"Wah, Minnalis, you meanie…," I wailed, reluctantly getting out of bed.

"I've already borrowed the kitchen to make breakfast, so let's head downstairs."

"Haah… Fine. Damn, this is just another thing to get revenge on her for."

…I'm not going to be having these dreams every night, am I?

"No way."

"Hmm? Master?"

"Nothing. Haah…"

I yawned, as if expelling all those negative thoughts, and I rubbed the sleep from my eyes.

Elmia, the City of Learning.

It was a city in the Orollea Kingdom that specialized in, obviously, schools and academies. All countries had cities with educational and research facilities of their own, but of them all, Elmia was famed for its creation of magic items, and the marquis was from a strong bloodline with powerful magical ability. The location was once a crossroads where many trade routes met, but over time, knowledge accumulated due to the rare artifacts that would pass through the area. Furthermore, many different alchemical catalysts could be found nearby, from monster materials to herbs, and so it was inevitable that research institutions would eventually start cropping up. The town that had started as a trade hub garnered a reputation for creating magic items, and this led to more and more adventurers flocking to the area to find the ingredients. The population rose, and the city flourished, as even more people moved into town seeking magic items and the theories behind their creation. Now, it was a city rivaling the capital itself. Eventually, the king officially recognized its influence in the pursuit of magical knowledge, and dubbed it "Elmia," which in the old tongue of Orollea meant "seeker of wisdom."

This was the city in which we had finally arrived only a few days ago.

"All right, here's your reward! Congratulations, you and your party have been promoted to E rank!"

"That's wonderful, thank you."

It was ten days after we arrived in Elmia, and I was by myself. I had spent the time slaying monsters and completing requests in order to raise our adventurer rank at Master's behest. I had just returned from hunting a rather fuzzy monster called the Lesser Ape.

"By the way, how is your partner doing? Kaito? I heard he got injured and was resting at the inn…"

"He's doing fine. His recovery is going well," I said with a smile. This receptionist was another beastfolk: a Vulpid, as evidenced by the fox ears atop her head, and recently I had gotten to know her quite well. Her boyfriend was an adventurer and she had picked up quite a few useful tips from him, so I often enjoyed coming to speak with her whenever I had a spare moment. Of course, what I was most inter-ested in was information that would aid us in our revenge.

I accepted my reward and left the guild, before heading to the marketplace to pick up some ingredients for dinner. In many ways, I was far more discerning on this battlefield than I was hunting mon-sters. This was going in Master's tummy, so it simply had to be up to snuff. As much as I hated to waste money, it was worth choosing the highest-quality ingredients I could find, within reason.

"Hello there, Minnalis. Picking up some food for your master?"

"Yes, that's right, ma'am. I'll take this and that… Oh, and that please, too. And could we maybe knock five copper pieces off the price?"

Of course, I was still going to get them as cheaply as possible. Why wouldn't I do that?

"Oh, you're a difficult one. Well, you did come by yesterday, too, so you can have a three-coin discount."

"Thank you very much. Here's the money."

I took a drawstring purse from my pack and handed over the coins.

These vegetables are of exceptional quality. The things you can find in a big city, I suppose.

I placed the produce in my bag, bowed to the greengrocer, and left. I'd long since forgotten how to put on a bright smile, but I'd keep that to myself if it helped me get revenge.

After that, I made my way back to the inn and headed up the stairs to our room. There, Master was lying on the bed, silent, his eyes closed. He had no wounds, in fact, he hadn't a single scratch. Report-ing him as such to the guild was his idea, to allow him to focus on this: his particular method of gathering information.

I ran my fingers through his soft, silky, black hair. I was tempted by all the things I wanted to do to his beautiful sleeping face, but I restrained myself. Right now, he would be able to feel me *on the other side.*

"Looks like you're not back yet, so I'll go make supper."

Somewhat reluctantly, I went downstairs and headed to the kitchen as always. Tonight's supper would be vegetable soup with bread. It had to be perfect.

Ever since we left the capital, Master had been giving me these things called "lessons," teaching me to swing a sword and the like. The most important thing, he always said, was gathering information and acting on it. So I decided to put those lessons to use and had been observing him for some time, trying to work out what kinds of food he liked without him noticing. That said, it was rather obvious when he liked something.

When talking about his favorite foods, the muscles in his face relaxed, and his voice became ever so slightly higher in pitch. When eating, he only filled his spoon with four fifths the usual amount, so as to savor the taste for longer. However, he still couldn't resist his favorites, so his chewing speed tended to increase, and the time between mouthfuls went down... *Oh, gosh, the subtle changes in his excitement are so cute, I can't stand it! It's some kind of trap, it must be! Why else would he be so innocent, so helpless, so vulnerable, while I'm trying my hardest to hold myself back?!*

"...Ahem. My thoughts got a little out of hand there."

I finished cutting up the fattybird I bought and moved on to the vegetables.

While striving to improve my cooking, I had also given some thought on how to perfect the spoon that would be going in Master's mouth. The size, the depth, the angles of the curves, the thickness of the handle... There was a lot more to it than I'd thought. After many overhauls, I was currently on model twenty-nine. As for the first twenty-eight models, I was keeping them for posterity. My favorite three were the very first, of course, model seventeen, as it was used for the longest before upgrading, and the freshest, model twenty-eight.

I yearned to add Master's bedding to my collection as well, but I knew it was wrong to steal from the inn. It was causing me a great deal of conflict. I had let it go in Golet, albeit not without tears, but this time I wondered if there wasn't some way it could be done...

Perhaps I could get away with switching mine and Master's bed-sheets once every couple of days without him noticing...

"Whoops, I've gone and gotten my head in the clouds again."

I shook my head to clear my mind and focused once more on the cooking before me. Master liked to have more vegetables than meat in his soup, and he preferred them chopped large enough that he could identify them.

I placed the vegetables into the boiling pot and skimmed off the scum from the top. Then I added in goat milk and butter. I let it simmer for a while, before finally adding salt to taste.

It was a recipe my mother had taught me, but apparently it was very similar to one of Master's favorite foods from his world, something called "cream stew."

"It's done. Now..."

I took a couple of slices of bread that had just finished lightly toasting and melted some cheese over their tops. As I gave a nod of satisfaction at the finished meal, the landlady came over.

"Oh, excellent work, as always. Is this for your master?"

"That's right, it is."

"...I know it's rough, but hang in there. Here, take this as well."

I wasn't sure why, but the landlady handed me a scarlet fruit called a kolin. Fruit was expensive, though, so I gratefully accepted it.

"Hmm? Oh, thank you..."

I supposed I might as well add it to the meal, so I sliced the fruit in half. Master had taught me about these things in his world called "apple rabbits" that you could make out of fruit like this, so I gave it a try.

Master is going to be eating this rabbit... Tee-hee, gosh, I like the sound of that...

I placed a lid on the pot, took the two slices of toast with cheese, and the kolin rabbits, and carried it all up the stairs to Master's room, since the bowls and spoons were in his pack. When I entered, Master was sitting up in bed.

"Ah, Minnalis, you're back."

"Yes, Master. I've made supper, too. Cream stew."

"Ooh, looks great, as always."

I made a portion with more vegetables in it and handed it to him.

""Thanks for the food.""

I performed the premeal gesture that Master had taught me and watched him closely as I reached for my serving. He seemed to enjoy his meal. That was nice. Also, I wanted that spoon. No, I wanted to *be* that spoon.

He tried to hide it, but I could see Master had been in a bad mood lately, ever since he went out hunting alone two days ago. I didn't know what happened out there, but it seemed to have angered him.

"What's the matter, Master? Did you not find anything out?"

Master had used the experience from those Redcaps to unlock another of his old abilities. It was a soul blade called the Mystic Blade of Soulfire that allowed him to become an invisible ghost whenever he liked. This ability allowed him to walk the streets and enter buildings unseen. Unfortunately, he couldn't control his physical body while doing this, so he stayed in his room at the inn as we made up a story about him being injured by monsters.

Whenever he went somewhere, Master tried to look happy, but

I could tell he was secretly feeling down. I've been watching him for so long now, after all. I imagined he was still depressed about being cheated for all that time in his previous life. Seeing him so sad made me so excited, my heart skipped a beat.

I'm sorry, I didn't mean that.

"Hmm? Nah, I did, I confirmed some of my suspicions. It's just..."

Master shuddered with disgust.

"I saw this awful scene at Eumis's mansion. It made me want to strangle her on the spot, and I didn't think it was possible to hate her any more than I already did. She's downright evil. I've only grown more convinced of that these past two days."

He always made this face when confronted with filth like her. He tapped the end of his spoon impatiently against the bottom of his bowl.

"Revenge isn't justice; it's only for my benefit. There's no point in getting revenge if it doesn't satisfy me, and I won't let anyone else have all the satisfaction, either. But if we could share it together..."

His dark smile crossed his lips.

"I think that would be more fun. I guess it depends on the person, though. Also, we'll probably have to play this one by ear a bit since I haven't written the script."

"...Can we save the riddles for another time, Master? I've been working hard by myself, finishing all those requests, and just today, I got us promoted to E rank. I want to be part of your revenge; I don't like being kept in suspense."

My task had been to gain experience in preparation for the real thing, and I had contented myself with it as penance for my past mistake. Even though Master had already said it was okay, I could see he knew it was weighing on my mind. But now, there was little left for me to do, and I wanted to move on to other things. It was hard, not being part of his vengeance. Perhaps it was time to end my self-imposed punishment. Any longer, and I'd risk being left behind.

That said, we're against one of his enemies this time, so it's only natural I should resign myself to a supporting role. Since we share revenge, though, my hatred for that woman is no less than his.

Yet I found it hard to stand up for myself. I was like putty in his hands. His warm, gentle hands…

Uh-oh, time to use my skill.

"Oh, sorry, I guess it must be pretty lame just watching me get all hyped up by myself. Sure, I'll fill you in… Actually, I'm surprised you got our rank raised already. Guess we don't need to take any more requests for a while. That's perfect timing, actually. It'll be time soon. I'll just check some things tomorrow and we can start deciding the basic outline."

"So…what did you find out in the end?"

"Well, Eumis is scum for sure, but her sister is, to put it arrogantly, worth a try."

"Eumis's…sister?"

"Yeah. I thought I'd gotten used to being unable to help people, but I guess not. I just can't stand to see what she's going through."

His voice was dark, pitch-black, and so quiet it seemed to tremble. Yet it didn't sound weak. In fact, it sounded so hot that I'd be burned if I were able to touch it.

But, Master. Her sister? You know what that means, don't you? A woman.

No, it's fine. I'm fine. Doesn't bother me at all. Hmph.

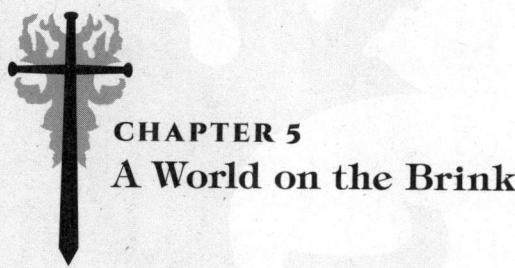

CHAPTER 5
A World on the Brink

"Miss Shuria, I've brought your breakfast."

"…Thank you."

At the knock and voice at the door, I placed a bookmark in my novel and closed it. The sun outside signaled that it was long past time for breakfast, but I'd been too engrossed by this story to put it down.

The volume I had just started reading was a romance novel, a passionate tale of forbidden love between a fey-blood earl and his slave girl, and of overcoming all the obstacles that stood between them. It seemed to be quite popular among the women of the city, and already I couldn't wait to see how it ended.

The, um…suggestive scenes were a bit too much, though, so I only skimmed over them…

"Breakfast is muroux steak, potota potage, and salad made with narna greens. For dessert, I have prepared frozen kolin, which I will bring to you later."

I got up from my chair in the corner of the room and sat at the dining table. Soriy was a maid working at the mansion, and she'd been looking after me over the last three years since I came to this city.

She rarely spoke more than necessary and never overstepped her

boundaries as a maid. She was always inscrutable, courteous, and kind.

"Can we eat together, Soriy?"

"I must decline, Miss. I am but a simple maid, and it would not befit my position to dine with the mistress's younger sister," she said, bowing her head.

Soriy was Eumis's retainer, and she had a lot of other work to do while looking after me. She had also grown up with my sister, and the two were old friends. I admit I was a little envious of the dashing figure she struck with her deep purple hair tied up at the back, her strikingly sharp features, and the womanly charm she seemed to exude from every one of her pores. As for me, my ancestral elven blood seemed to run strong, and though I was already fourteen years of age, my body was barely more developed than a child's. I would have liked to at least have a little of her bust. And height.

"The chef has adjusted the seasoning. Is it to your liking, Miss?"

"It's very nice. So much so, I feel guilty eating it alone."

"I see. I will pass on your compliments to the chef."

After I had finished my dessert and put the somewhat formal meal behind me, I called Soriy back to my room to take away my empty plates.

"Um… Do you have the…?"

"Ah, your new stuffed toy. Wait here just a second."

Soriy left the room and came back with a large doll of a bear monster.

"I hope I bought the right one."

"…Thank you."

It had patchwork fur of yellow and red, a zipper mouth, and two brown buttons for eyes. It was very cute. I took the bear and cuddled it in my arms. The expensive cloth and cotton felt so soft against my skin.

"We shall wait outside. If you have need of anything, simply call." Then, as always, she added, "Now, excuse me, Miss Shuria," and left the room as neatly as a ballerina.

I stroked and nuzzled the new toy and rolled around with it on the bed to my heart's content. Then I placed it alongside all the others.

"I'll put you here. You're my new favorite," I cooed, placing the bear by the pillow of my enormous bed.

"...Now, time to begin," I said aloud, clenching my fists. It was time for my daily workout routine.

I was just a simple village girl, unsuited to the life of an aristocrat. Particularly the extravagant meals. If I wasn't careful, I was sure I would swell up like a balloon in no time at all. Even more so because I had to stay in this room all the time. Physical activity also helped me combat the stress and lack of exercise caused by staying indoors. However, for some reason, I didn't seem to put on a single ounce of muscle. Was this due to my elf blood, too? Not that I would wish for a six-pack or anything.

After my morning sweat, I hopped into my en suite shower to freshen up. There were no such luxuries in the village; instead, we bathed in the river during the day while the water was still warm. I was going to be spoiled rotten here. I was never going to be able to go back. But it felt so good...

"...Ahhh, that was nice."

"My, Shuria, you're indecent."

"E-Eumis?!"

When I got out of the bath, my sister was sitting in my favorite seat by the window. A smile passed across her noble features, and her dark green hair, like fresh leaves, glittered in the sun filtering in through the window. I, on the other hand, was dressed only in a bath towel.

"I-I'm sorry," I squealed, pulling on my clothes.

"Oh, you don't need to rush on my account. I must have come at the wrong time, that's all."

"Th-that's not true, Eumis, I know you're always so busy..."

I made myself decent and sat down across from her.

"I bought some delicious cakes today, and I thought we might share them. Also, I brought you your letter."

"Thank you so much!"

I took the letter and its attached voice playback device with care, and I placed them on my desk. As much as I wanted to listen to it right away, Eumis deserved my full attention while she was here.

"This will be the final letter," she said. "Very soon the ritual will be complete, and you will be able to talk to your family directly."

"These letters have been a blessing. Thank you so much!"

"Don't mention it. You must have been lonely these past three years. Besides, it was my grandmother who invented the voice playback device. Using a few a month for personal matters is no big deal."

She gave another charming smile. No matter how many times I saw it, it always fascinated me.

"Well then, shall we dive in? The tea will get cold."

"Yes, please!"

I had a relaxing drink with Eumis. My sister was always busy, so we didn't spend much time together, but she occasionally came to visit me in my room when she could.

It had only been three years since we met, but already my sister meant the world to me. She was kind and gentle, and I respected her very much.

Three years ago, I learned that Eumis was my big sister. I was born and raised in a village surrounded by trees at the foot of a mountain northeast of Elmia. There, it was just the three of us: my mother, my little sister, and me. We had no father, and mother never once spoke of him. Still, we never went hungry, due to the magic granted to me by my elven blood.

My mother told me she was descended from elves, and perhaps this explained my golden hair, my pale skin, my slow growth, and my pointy ears. I also possessed an intrinsic ability, "Scarlet Eyes," that allowed me to see raw mana. It came in very handy when casting spells.

My village was founded by old adventurers, and there was no discrimination against demihumans there. We weren't rich, but we lived in harmony, and I was able to make a little money by working as an adventurer.

We didn't have much, but we were happy.

But those times didn't last forever.

My sister Shelmie fell ill. It wasn't fatal, but it left her in great pain, and we could not afford the cure. I worked hard so I could save up the money to buy it, but the price was still far out of our reach. I was even thinking about selling myself off, when Eumis came to our village.

She told me my mother had once been a maid at the Elmia mansion and that I was born of the master's affair. It was when she was pregnant with Shelmie that the master's wife found out, and he was forced to pay my mother off and send her away. With a young me in tow, she eventually ended up in this village.

That made Eumis our half sister. She came to our village because of the magic power I possessed. Using a special technique, she could transfer my magical ability to herself. I would lose the ability to cast magic, but in return, we were offered enough money to afford the cure for Shelmie and live the rest of our lives without hardship.

I jumped at the offer without a second thought. It was a little sad I couldn't use magic anymore, but it was a small price to pay to allow the three of us to live happily together once more. I watched my sister drink the potion and be cured, and then I was taken to the Elmia estate.

I was told the ritual had a lot of rules. I had to be confined to a single room of the mansion and was told I could not make contact with any other blood relatives besides Eumis, which meant I was unable to see my family.

I was lonely, but Eumis looked after me. She allowed them to send me letters using her voice playback device, since neither my mother nor sister could write, and she even spent time with me and brought me fancy cakes like today. She helped me learn to read and asked Soriy to bring me my favorite toys and novels to help combat the boredom.

She was always kept busy acting in the master's place and researching magic items at the academy. Despite that, she made sure to visit me whenever she could. It wasn't long before I began to think of her as my real elder sister.

Once the ritual was complete, my mother and Shelmie would be brought to live in the city with me. As for the master, he was currently living with his wife in the capital, leaving Eumis to take over his duties, so it was safe for us to live here, and I would be allowed to visit the mansion whenever I liked.

Her gentle smile always put my heart at ease, and I was eternally grateful for all she had done for me.

Very soon, I would be able to meet my family again. There were things I couldn't tell by voice alone. How much had Shelmie grown? Unlike me, the elf blood was not very prominent in her. She might even be taller than me now. I couldn't wait to try my mother's freshly baked ricolle pies again. I'm sure Eumis would love them, too. The four of us could enjoy tea and cakes together.

Ahhh, I'm the luckiest girl in the world.

My life was happy. Every day was the same, but they were filled with joy.

Then all of a sudden, a strange ghost appeared in the room.

No, not a ghost…a spirit.

"*Phew.* The grand chamberlain sure likes to work us to the bone."

"That he does."

"Hey, don't let her catch you saying that or we'll all be in trouble!"

""We knooow!""

The three maids chatted as they tossed their bags of household waste into the large container outside.

I'll be letting myself in, if you don't mind.

While they were distracted, I entered the mansion through the back door. Normally, I could pass through walls while in this ghostly state, but the walls of the Elmia mansion were fortified with powerful wards that blocked me. The Mystic Blade of Soulfire transformed me into a being of pure mana, so that physical defenses were pretty much... No, scratch that, they were entirely useless, but there was very little I could do against magical defenses, so this was the easiest way for me to enter the mansion.

When I did, I detected Eumis's special intruder-detecting wards. If I triggered them, Eumis would know I was here immediately, and it would summon half a dozen golems to capture and restrain me.

However, I already knew about her wards and how they worked from the first time, and so I knew that in this form, I had nothing to worry about from even the greatest of the mansion's security measures. The only things that could possibly detect me while I was invisible and incorporeal were the extremely advanced skill "Mind's Eye" and the intrinsic ability Scarlet Eyes.

But I knew she didn't have Mind's Eye yet, because I was the one who'd taught her it.

Come to think of it, this is the first time I've actually been here.

Expensive furnishings lined the corridors, and the carpets

beneath my ghostly feet looked soft, even though I couldn't feel them in this form.

Now, where should I begin?

I was here to find out the best way to make Eumis suffer. I already knew she wanted to invent a new magic item that would secure a place for her name on the stone monument of Elmia. In fact, she was obsessed with the idea. Her eyes, filled with madness when she thought about that dream, were now seared into my memory.

However, I never understood why it was so important to her. It had been a dream of hers since she was very young, sure. But on that day, I saw in her eyes something more. There was a practical reason behind her wish, I was sure of it. My primary goal here was to find out what that was, and if I could uncover a weakness or two of hers while I was at it, so much the better.

If all I wanted was to tear her limb from limb, I could do that whenever I liked.

I guess I'll look for a study or something.

If Eumis's secrets were anywhere, they would be there. If I could find an old diary or something similar, I might learn something about her unfathomable desire.

It was normal for such rooms to be on the upper floors, near the center of the building, so that's where I headed. The mansion was enormous, hardly surprising considering it was the home of a lord's daughter.

As I passed a maid on the staircase, she suddenly stopped.

"Hmm? What was that…?"

She turned back in my direction, her body tense. She seemed to be in her twenties, her deep violet hair tied up in a ponytail, and she peered back in my direction, confused.

Grh…did she notice me?!

Soriy Lurel

Lv23

Age 23 • Female • Human

HP: 310/310   MP: 222/222

Strength: 183   Stamina: 143

Vitality: 144   Agility: 208

Magic: 119   Resistance: 122

Intrinsic Abilities: Intuition
Skills: Resist Pain Lv 2, Notice Lv 1,
Stealth Lv 1, Carve Lv 3,
Darkvision Lv 3, Sword Lv 2, Iron Mask Lv 1,
Reaction Time Lv 1
Status: OK

I quickly checked her status, but I didn't find any skill that would allow her to see me. It must have been her intrinsic ability, Intuition, that tipped her off.

"...Must be my imagination..."

The maid called Soriy looked around curiously, but unable to find anything, continued on down the stairs.

Wait! There she is!!

"Ah, Mistress. I see you've returned."

"Indeed I have, Soriy."

At the bottom of the stairs stood that wretched louse Eumis.

"I assumed you would be spending the day at the office today," said Soriy.

"I just came back home to rest, and while I'm here, there are some papers I need to stamp. They should arrive any moment, so until then, why don't you take a break with me? I'll be in my bedroom. Could I trust you to bring the usual stuff?"

"Y-yes, ma'am. I'll go fetch it now."

"Tee-hee-hee... I'll see you there, then."

Hmm...this is my chance to see what they get up to in private.

Just as I thought I'd made a blunder, I came across a gold mine of potential information. Watching the maid talk reminded me who she was. This woman was Eumis's trusted retainer. When Eumis was away from the estate—and her responsibilities fell to her younger, elven-blood sister—it was Soriy who advised her in that capacity. Even now, she must have some knowledge of the inner workings of the estate, and she certainly knew a lot about Eumis. I might learn something of her true nature if I sat in on their little break time and listened to their chatter.

I decided to follow up on this lead before I searched the upper floor. A grin crept across my lips as I trailed behind them.

...I thought I might overhear something juicy, like problems they were having, people they didn't like. I wasn't prepared in the slightest for this.

I mean, what the hell am I seeing?

"Mmah... Hee-hee-hee...this is the spot, huh, Soriy?"

"Aahn! N-not there, Miss Eumis... Aaah! Ahhh...mm... Mmm-hmm...!"

"Ah, you sound so cute, Soriy. You can moan louder if you want, you know?"

"Mmh... Aaaah!"

Why do I have to watch these two pigs mating...?! Ugh!

Hmm, I suppose it's not technically "mating" if they're the same gender. If it were any other duo of pretty girls in this situation, I'd thank my lucky stars, but to me, this pairing was less like a porno and more like a horror movie. I felt sick.

By the way, "the usual stuff" turned out to be some kind of sticky lotion. They were rubbing it all over their hides like slimy little maggots.

Hmm, but I guess I did learn something. Eumis is actually a lesbian.

So this is what they did behind closed doors. The pervasive, sickly odor of incense filled the room.

I had always wondered why she never seemed to react at all to the suitors who came to court her. Some of them were rather handsome men, even by this world's standards. This explains it. The pig was only ever interested in girls.

"Aahhh...mmm... Mmm!"

Okay, that's enough. I can't take it anymore...

It felt like I was taking psychic damage just standing here. A second longer and I was going to be forcibly sent back to my real body.

I slipped out, phasing through the closed door, still reeling from the sight.

Time to pull myself together. I need to find a study.

Those two seemed to be keeping themselves occupied, so I could probably get away with making myself partially corporeal if it made things easier. Shaking my head to remove the images I had just seen from my brain, I headed up the stairs. I was checking all the various rooms one by one when I hit upon something promising.

This is the only room with two layers of physical defenses... There's an item stopping me from detecting what's inside, but I can tell there's some sort of magic circle surrounding the whole room.

It wouldn't be easy to get inside, but that just meant there must be something in there worth hiding. The magic circle probably wasn't a detection spell, since it would conflict with the anti-detection magic item. It was probably something designed to inflict harm on intruders.

They really didn't want people getting in here. The physical defenses were no threat to me while I was incorporeal, so the only thing I had to worry about was the magic circle which covered the whole room. That said, I was going to have to enter it to find out what I was dealing with, so I covered my ghostly body with a thin layer of mana to raise my magical resistance. With this in place, I would have a few seconds before the magic circle's effect, whatever it was, acted upon me. That would buy me enough time to figure out what it was and, if necessary, get out again while I thought up a plan.

So what secrets are you hiding in here?

I passed through the door and entered the room. I was prepared for any magical trap I might activate. What I was not prepared for, however, was what I saw. It wasn't a study at all. There were stuffed toys everywhere, and nothing like a large desk where somebody might work. It just looked like a bedroom, and there was someone inside. It was Eumis's sister.

I had considered using her to exact my vengeance against Eumis, but now that I was in her room, there was something very strange.

Hold on, what the hell…? What does this mean? This mana…it's a Contract spell. What is it doing here…?

The magic circle was not, as I had surmised, for repelling intruders. Its purpose was to apply a *curse* to something specific in the room.

And following the mana leads me to her. The curse is on Eumis's sister. What is going on here?

Contract magic was usually the exclusive domain of demons. Their particular brand of mana was required in order to activate the spell, though it could be maintained after that without it.

It was strange enough for such a spell to be hidden in the Elmia household in the first place, but that the magic circle maintaining it was focused on Eumis's own sister was simply baffling.

First things first, I should use my Appraise skill on the magic circle to learn more, I thought, when suddenly…

"…"

Hmm…?

The girl sitting by the window, an open letter in her hand, was staring right at me in amazement, her eyes a brilliant crimson.

…Crimson? Ah, crap, don't tell me…

I tried moving left and right, and the girl followed my movements. Her eyes went wide in disbelief.

Harboring one last glimmer of hope, I turned my Appraise skill upon the girl, only for those hopes to be dashed.

"…Are you a ghost?"

…This day is just full of surprises.

Shuria
Lv31

Age 14 • Female • Human
(Elf Blood)

HP: 332/332   MP: 525/525

Strength: 133   Stamina: 213

Vitality: 194   Agility: 288

Magic: 549   Resistance: 522

Intrinsic Abilities: Scarlet Eyes

Skills: Notice Lv 1, Stealth Lv 1,

Water Magic Lv 1, Wind Magic Lv 1,

Meditate Lv 3, Carve Lv 3

Status: OK (Bound by Contract)

Why does she have Scarlet Eyes?

Turns out there was an awful lot going on in this mansion that I didn't know about. It was particularly strange because I had met this girl before, and she never had red eyes.

Did I misremember things...? No, she had green eyes, I'm sure of it.

Intrinsic abilities were generally fixed at birth, and people with the Scarlet Eyes ability all had red eyes. Except I distinctly remembered her having green eyes before. It wasn't easy to forget seeing that small elven girl on the battlefield the first time I fought the horde here.

If only I had her data from last time still stored in the Eight-Eyed Sword of Clarity, I could be sure, but unfortunately, it was only after I met her that I'd acquired that soul blade.

In any case, it doesn't seem like she's trying to raise the alarm.

I was about to run away, but her behavior gave me pause.

This was how I could hit Eumis where it hurts. I knew it. It was mostly conjecture at this point, but this had to lead me to an aspect of Eumis I didn't see the first time.

The problem now is what exactly do I do here?

"Be not afraid. I come in...peace? I don't suppose that's very convincing."

I needed to materialize a little in order to talk. I was only creating a false body out of mana, though. My real body was, of course, still back at the inn. Hence, it was a little weaker than a real human body. To her Scarlet Eyes, I would look exactly the same, but at least by giving myself a voice, I might appear a little less creepy. Right now, I wanted to buy time until I could figure out exactly what was going on here.

"...You're not a ghost. You're...a spirit?"

"Er...what? No, I...what?"

Something seemed to resonate with the young girl—though I

wasn't sure exactly what—and she hopped out of her seat and crossed the room toward me. Her facial expression didn't change, but she seemed intensely curious about me.

"Wow. I've never seen a spirit before, not even in the forest! To think I would see one here…"

She was like a teenage schoolgirl meeting her favorite pop star. I could almost see the sparkle in her eyes.

"I've got so many things I want to ask a spirit. Where do you come from? Is it the forest outside the city? What do you eat?"

"Huh? No, you've got it all wrong. I'm not really a…"

What the hell is going on? Was my memory always this bad?

The Shuria I remembered was never this talkative. She was always emotionless, only ever answering questions with "yes" or "no." I had tried talking to her a few times, but not once had she ever struck up a conversation in return. She was like a doll. At least, that's how I remembered her.

So what is this? It wouldn't be wrong to still call her a quiet girl, for sure. But there was emotion behind her actions, and that was something I had never seen before.

Perhaps she just really liked spirits that much. Was that possible?

"Uh-um, and also…," she stammered.

"Hold on, calm down— Uh…"

"Ee…"

As the restless girl instinctively grabbed my hand, my arm fell off. Right now, I might as well have been made of polystyrene. I suppose the shaking was too much for my poor shoulder.

"Ee…eh…oh…"

"Um… You okay?"

Being only a temporary body, it didn't hurt me at all, and I could always just make another one. The girl, however, was clearly disturbed by the sight. I could almost see her soul leaving her body. I waved my reconstructed hand in front of her eyes to show that everything was fine, but…

"Uhhh…"

"Nope, she's a goner."

I sighed and waited for her to return to the world of the living.

It took the girl a few minutes to come back to her senses. We sat across from each other at the large table in the center of the room.

"…I'm sorry. That was so rude of me… My name's Shuria, by the way. Is your arm all better now?"

"Yeah, I'm fine. My body's mostly just made of mana, anyway."

"…Spirits sure are something."

"Yeah…whatever, let's just go with that."

It seemed she was more willing to talk if I let her believe I was a spirit. I used to know a priest on Earth. Perhaps I should try talking a bit more like him.

"…Why did you come here? Is there something you have to do?"

"I wanted to ask you something, um…my little lost lamb."

"Shuria. Please call me Shuria."

"…Right. Shuria. You can see the magic circle in this room, can't you? You know it's centered on you, right?"

While Shuria was having an out-of-body experience of her own, I had taken the opportunity to examine the magic circle for myself.

Here's what it said:

==

Six-Colored Hexing Circle of Transference

By keeping the target within the confines of the Hexing Circle, the target's skills and affinities in Fire, Water, Wind, Earth, Light, and Dark magic can be transferred to a second target.

Once the hex is 50% complete, the transferred skills and affinities manifest in the beneficiary. Note that in order for the hex to be effective, the target and beneficiary must share a soul compatibility of blood-relation class.

Target: Shuria   Beneficiary: Eumis Elmia

Hex progression: 96% (Time remaining: 7 days)

===

It was quite a nasty curse. It took away not only your skill proficiencies but also your affinities. That meant that you couldn't even build your skills back up afterward. Essentially, it made you unable to cast magic ever again.

I looked at her with my advanced Appraise skill, and her six elemental affinities were almost completely gone. Given her elven blood, they ought to have been pretty high. Her skill proficiencies, too, were way too low compared to her current level.

Contract spells of this type—ones that stole affinities and skills pretty closely linked to the target's soul—took a considerable amount of time to complete, and it was clear that this Shuria girl had been confined to this room for a very long time indeed.

"This is so that I can give my talent for magic to Eumis. There are a lot of things in this world that I don't understand."

I don't think there are many people who do understand these kinds of spells. They're evil curses, used only by demons. But...

With her Scarlet Eyes, she could see the mana leaving her body, and thanks to the passive effect of the Mystic Blade of Soulfire, I could see raw mana, too. It was not a pleasant sight. How could she stay so happy?

"Why would you do such a thing...?"

"My sister Shelmie. She was sick. I agreed to give up my magic so that we could afford the magic potion to cure her disease."

Her sister? I never knew Eumis had another sister.

"Huh. But how is that your price to pay? Shelmie is your sister, right? Doesn't that make her Eumis's sister, too?"

"We are only half related to Eumis. We grew up apart from her. We couldn't expect to be given such a large sum for free simply because we were of the same blood."

"And you're okay with this?"

"Yes. I'm sad I won't be able to use magic anymore, but she's paying me enough to afford the magic potion and live comfortably with my family for the rest of our lives. I only ever used my magic as a means to survive, anyway. Besides," she continued, "Eumis told me it would help her achieve her dream. I'm happy to give up my magic power if it is of use to her."

"I see. You must really love your sister."

"I do!" she said, without hesitation. "Eumis is amazing! She works so hard, and she handles her father's work even though she's only a few years older than me…!"

She smiled softly as she spoke, a rare change of expression. It was a testament to her love. I smiled back, but the shutters had already clapped over my ears. I was no longer listening, and in the back of my mind, the gears were turning.

So in order to advance her research, she took the magical ability of her elf-blood sister. And in return for taking away her means of earning a living, Eumis granted Shuria not only the magic potion to cure her sister's illness, but also enough money to live out the rest of her and her family's lives…

That explained why Eumis's magical affinities were always much higher than a normal human's should have been. But if that was all there was to it, there wasn't much left to say. I may have found out why her magic was so strong, but there was nothing I could do to reverse the hex at this point. But that wasn't the end of the story.

First, I had to find out why Eumis knew about this spell in the first place, and how she'd cast it.

And second, I had to work out why the Shuria sitting before me now differed to the one in my memories.

Also, it was probably just me being pessimistic, but I couldn't shake the bad feeling that something else was wrong. The Shuria I remember seemed to have no emotions at all. Though she may have been reserved right now, she definitely exhibited her feelings. There was no question about it.

I felt a discomfort sticking into my throat like pins. It felt like any moment, everything was going to fall into place, and there was nothing I could do to stop it.

It was then that I heard a voice.

"—ria, have you been well?"

"H-huh? Oh!"

Hmm? What's that?

I turned toward the source, only to find it was coming from a letter on the desk by the window. It was the one Shuria was opening when I entered the room. The paper was marked with the pale blue crest of the Elmia marquis. I was familiar with how the recording device attached to it worked. You could record messages into it and play them back at any time with a simple touch.

"Ah, this flower must have fallen onto the page," guessed Shuria. I looked to see that one of the pretty purple and yellow flowers from a potted plant atop the desk had fallen from its stem and onto the paper itself. That must have activated the device.

"*The Evening Calms in your garden have sprouted again. Shelmie's been taking good care of them this year.*"

What's wrong? I thought. *Why do I feel so…?*

"Is that your mother?"

The voice I heard belonged to a young woman. Yet there was

something off about it I couldn't quite place, and it sounded as if I'd heard it somewhere before.

"Yes. Oh, and this is my sister Shelmie."

"Have you been well, sister? You aren't sick, are you? Are you eating and sleeping well? I feel so much better. I know you always say you're doing fine, but I worry about you having trouble adjusting to your new life. I've been taking care of the flowers you planted. They tell me we'll soon be able to meet again. I'm looking forward to it so much."

"Shelmie... She's my little sister, but she always makes fun of me."

"Ah-ha-ha...she sounds like a great sibling to me."

Shuria even blushed a little in embarrassment. The girl in the letter reminded me of my own sister back home. She always had her act together, much more so than I ever did. She always fussed over me and told me what to do as well.

Even as I lingered in recollection, I noticed this voice also sounded off. I mean, it was that of a young girl, higher in pitch than the previous voice, but something still didn't seem right about it.

...I know. There's no emotion behind their words at all.

It wasn't as though they were chanting in monotone; it wasn't that obvious. But there was none of the intonation, inflection, rises and falls of pitch that people usually used when they spoke. It was fixed, like a machine was talking instead of a human. Yeah, as if the voices I remembered were...

As soon as I realized the significance of what I was hearing, I felt a *click* in the back of my head, as the last piece of the puzzle fell into place. The gears started to turn as I pieced together my theory.

...Ha-ha. I see. It all makes sense now. I suppose it is that easy to fool someone after all.

Shuria must have noticed it, too, that the voices of her family sounded different to how she remembered. But if Eumis told her that's just how it worked, then why wouldn't Shuria believe her? What reason would she have not to trust her dear sister?

As for the Contract spell... Ah, I know what she must have used. They were created using demon magic, after all. For the cost...well, that part is obvious. And then if I think about the sorts of things Eumis might do, the rest all comes together.

As soon as the final image formed in my mind, I began to feel dizzy. *...Oh. This again.*

The whole thing had nothing to do with me, and yet it reminded me so much of myself that the dark flame inside me suddenly flared out of control, as if it had been doused in black, tarry oil.

"Can I just ask you something?"

"...?"

The letter had ended, and Shuria was carefully folding it back up when I called out to her.

"That flower that landed on the letter. Was it by any chance the same as those flowers your family mentioned?"

"Yes. They are extremely vigorous flowers, though they tend not to grow in great numbers."

"I see. They're very pretty," I said, before standing up from the table. "I should get going. Please don't tell anybody that you saw me. I wasn't really supposed to come and talk to you."

"R-really? Okay, I'll keep it a secret!"

Shuria clenched her fists. Just like when she first saw me, I could somehow see the stars in her eyes despite her expression barely changing at all. I could probably trust that she wouldn't tell Eumis about me now.

"Um... Can I ask you your name, Mr. Spirit?"

"Sure. My name's Kaito."

"Kaito... Um...will I ever see you again?"

"Yeah, I think you will."

With that, I returned fully to my spectral form, and ended the Mystic Blade of Soulfire's effect.

"Man... This world really is nothing but trash."

After a short floaty feeling similar to using a teleportation stone, I arrived in my bed at the inn. Minnalis had not yet returned.

"Haah... Maybe I should go."

The heat inside me boiled and seethed. Right now, I could find the perfect opponent on which to vent my anger. I'd been hoping to go there in a few days with Minnalis and let her practice fighting against a large horde. I suppose it just wasn't meant to be. At least I'd get the chance to practice my secret technique. I still needed to find out how effective it'd be when I used it against Eumis. Also...

Argh, dammit. I couldn't pretend anymore. There was no rational reason behind it. I just wanted to go wild or else I'd lose my damn mind. Right now, I was a pent-up ball of fire with nowhere to go.

"Glug-glug. Haah."

I downed a potion to restore the MP I used up with the Mystic Blade of Soulfire, then I left the inn and headed to the east gate. There, I slipped off the beaten path and went down a woodland trail by myself.

Logically, I knew that this time would be better spent researching my enemy. There were still some things I was uncertain about, I realized that. It's just, if I ran into her again there in the mansion, I don't know if I'd have been able to hold myself back.

"Ah, they're in there. Perfect chance to let off some steam and practice my secret technique."

I stood before the forest. Within it, I sensed a writhing mass of monsters, of far greater numbers than when I went against Zui-ly's party. In only a few more days, they'd spill out of the forest and attack the city.

My lips curled up into a smile. When it came to venting my uncontrollable rage, the more the merrier. I sauntered gleefully into the forest, barely making it ten paces before a pair of goblins leaped out at me. Conjuring the Soul Blade of Beginnings in my right hand, and the Nephrite Blade of Verdure in my left, I sliced them both cleanly in two.

""Grah-grah-grah?!""

"Sorry. It's not you guys I have a problem with."

Tying the Nephrite Blade of Verdure to my hip by its tassel, I took the Holy Sword of Retribution in my left hand.

"Grah!!" "Bregh?!" "Kraugh?!" "Gr-gah!!" "Brooouh..." "Gah?!"

"It's no use. It's still not enough. But I can't let my partner see me like this."

In the blink of an eye, I flitted from spot to spot, annihilating the monsters all around me, while turning and slicing the ones that attempted to flank me. The forest was filled with the screams of dying monsters, so much so that my ears were beginning to go crazy.

"I just need to let out some stress..."

In the few minutes since I entered the forest, I had slaughtered all the monsters found in the outer reaches. Detecting an even greater presence lurking ahead, I approached a clearing about the size of a gymnasium, where a great number of people must have cut down the trees to set up camp. There I found many monsters: Redcaps, hobgoblins, Sword Goblins, Red Boars, Big Boars, orcs, High Orcs, trolls.

They all turned and glared at me. There were easily about a hundred of them.

Ah, maybe now I can finally fight to my heart's content.

"Glug, glug, haah."

I took another MP potion, and tossed the empty bottle aside, then immediately leaped into the crowd of monsters.

"Gragh?!" "Gu-guh!!" "Goragh!!"

I stabbed the three closest to me with a single thrust and pulled out my sword, soaking the ground in their blood.

"...so much for blowing off steam by killing you."

With that, I released the brakes on my body and forced my gears into overdrive.

"Ha-ha!! Aha-ha-ha-ha-ha-ha!!"

My blade showed not a drop of mercy. Heads flew, blood spurted. I pierced organs and crushed necks.

"Die! Ahhh, this is good! Marvelous!"

The blood went to my head and made me giddy. A feeling almost like being drunk rose up and washed away my thoughts. No emotion, no doubt. My whole mind was devoted to murder. I loved them. I loved these monsters I could slaughter without feeling guilty.

"Ha-ha! Aha-ha-ha-ha!!"

The mad laughter flowed from me almost unconsciously. It was a rampage, but it was a righteous one.

This was no careful killing, no pinpoint strikes to the vitals. I was just swinging my sword with enough force to tear them messily apart. By the time I was halfway done, the bodies formed a pile, and blood soaked the soil.

Before long, the only thing there that still drew breath was me.

"Haah...haah...hooo..."

I took a deep sigh, as if expelling the leftover heat. All that remained within me was a pile of smoldering embers and a great feeling of emptiness.

The words poured from my lips. "Why do I only ever find out once it's too late?"

You were right, Leticia. There are beautiful things in this world. But there are also nasty things, dirty things. Way more of them than either of us ever imagined.

My fists were clenched so tightly my fingernails drew blood from my palms. This was the highest form of self-deceit. I knew that. If there were anything I could do, I could make it part of my revenge, turn it to my advantage. But there wasn't, and still I sympathized with her. I pitied her. I saw myself in her. And I decided to voice the complaints I've been bottling up inside me this whole time.

"...Why do I only ever start from the point of no return?"

I had always told myself thinking about it wouldn't help, but it was just an excuse. I was like a crying child throwing a tantrum, knowing I couldn't have what I wanted but still refusing to accept it.

If this was really a do-over, then why was I only brought back to the moment I arrived? From that point on, it was already too late. I had already lost everything by then.

"Ha-ha...pathetic."

I knew I ought to be grateful. It was a miracle I had been given another opportunity to exact my vengeance. The world didn't revolve around me. It didn't care one iota about me and my problems, and even though I'd gotten a second chance, it didn't mean I was special. My do over was given to me not because I'd sworn revenge, or because I'd wished for it. It was something the Goddess or whoever gave to everybody.

Yet I couldn't get it out of my head. I couldn't help but scream and wail at how unfair and pathetic it all was.

That's why I had to unload my anger. Because it was something I could never talk about. It was a weakness of mine. My greatest weakness. And the sight of that girl hit me right where it hurts.

"I really...don't want anyone to ever see me in this miserable state."

I wanted to go back. I wanted to go back so much I could scream. It was pathetic. Was that any way for an avenger to act?

"I'll kill them. I don't care anymore what happens. I have to trample them into the ground and slaughter them."

That was all I could think about now. This was the path I had chosen, the only way I could be satisfied. My final complaint purged the impurities from within me, leaving only a pure, black, cold flame of vengeance. Kill them all. The oath that brought my soul back to life.

My prey had been brought before me. I didn't have time to wallow in regret. I had to make her suffer. Tear away at her heart and mind until nothing remained but despair. And then I'd kill her.

When I carried out my revenge, I needed my heart to contain nothing but vengeance. Revenge was sweet, a loving but jealous mistress. She would not permit me to look away.

"Haah... I think that helped me calm down a bit."

In the aftermath of my rampage, I felt my worries and anger slip away, as if sinking to the bed of a deep lake.

"Ha-ha-ha... Look at me now. This is just laughable..."

I realized I was utterly drenched from head to toe in monster blood. It was disgusting.

I still had around 30 percent of my MP remaining, but I was already feeling drunk from the sudden loss. It was a feeling I usually found unpleasant, but now it felt somehow comforting.

That took longer than I expected, and I even used all the techniques I had access to right now. I'm just not up to where I was before yet.

Thinking this, I took a flask of water from my pack and held it high above my head, dousing myself in water to wash away the blood. As the cold water hit my skin, I remembered Shuria's words.

"Kaito... Um...will I ever see you again?"

"Yeah, you will. I'll make sure of it," I vowed.

I will drag you from that world, through a sea of needles, into the light. And if you wish, I will show you the way from there.

Like the devil himself.

"...All right."

Shaking the water off me like a dog, I stretched my limbs and cracked my neck.

"I'm hungry. And tired. I wanna go to bed...," I groaned, rubbing my rumbling belly.

The hour was not yet right for afternoon tea, but although I had enjoyed quite a hearty lunch, I was already starving, as if I had not eaten all day. In addition, the use of my secret technique had drained my MP and left me totally exhausted. Trying to ignore the pervasive smell of blood, I pulled from my pack a couple of pieces of dried meat I wouldn't need to cook. Chewing on them, I reluctantly decided I really ought to do something about the state I'd left the forest in, and summoned Slimo to take care of the bodies. The smell would have to remain. There was nothing I could do about that.

Then, with no further reason to loiter in the forest, I started walking, greedily wolfing down the meat as I tried to find somewhere that didn't smell quite so foul.

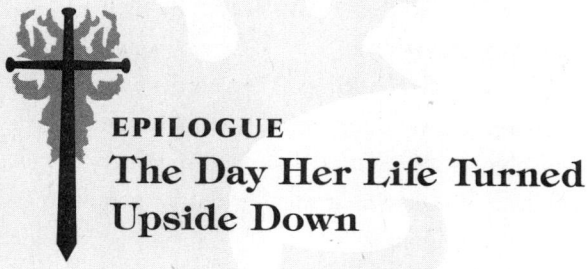

EPILOGUE
The Day Her Life Turned Upside Down

Yes, this is a story about the day her life turned upside down. A day that started like any other, the sun shining brightly in the sky; the birds singing. To everyone else, the day would continue like any other, too, until the streets sank back into the vermilion light of dusk.

But she would remember that day forever, right up until the moment she expired...or even beyond.

"Kaito didn't come back today, either."

I sighed deeply, blowing bubbles in the bathtub. It had been four days since the spirit, Kaito, passed through my door and appeared in my room. I was really surprised. I never thought the day would come when I would get to meet a real live spirit.

There was a story my mother used to tell me when I was younger, about a half-elf girl and a light spirit who lived inside a doll. They ran into problems, but they always overcame them by working together, and they lived happily ever after.

That was just a story, though. I'm not a half elf; I only have elven blood in my veins. And I'm not saying I want to spend my whole life with a spirit. I just want to talk to them. And maybe be their friend.

"...Maybe I was acting *too* friendly."

Spirits were whimsical and fickle beings. They hardly ever showed themselves to people at all. Even if one showed up in a human dwelling, nobody would be able to see it unless they had my Scarlet Eyes, or if it chose to reveal itself. Otherwise, it was normal for people to go their whole lives without seeing one at all.

"...Next time, I'll make sure to ask him if he wants to be my friend."

Apparently, there were special items that could summon spirits, but they were so rare and expensive barely anybody could get their hands on them. Eumis had one, though, but she couldn't show it to me because it was "delicate."

Maybe he found me boring. I'm not good at keeping a conversation going, I thought, as I splashed about in the tub.

It was the first time I had seen a spirit. At first, I thought it was a ghost, but it must have been a spirit because he was able to materialize and let me touch him.

"I'll have to think of something more interesting to say for next time."

I stood up out of the bath and dried myself off, before pulling on my pajamas and rubbing my hair with a towel. Then I poured myself a cup of water from the jug provided in my room, and holding it in both hands, drank it dry in three gulps. When I lived in the village, the man next door told me this is what you do when you get out of the bath. Actually, you were supposed to put one hand on your hip, too, but my mother got angry when she saw me doing that, so I'd always done it like this instead.

Then, all warm from the bath, I crawled under the covers and snuggled up in bed.

According to Eumis, there were only a few more days before the spell would be complete. Then I would say good-bye to this bed, to this room. She said I could keep my stuffed toys, but it was still a little sad.

However, it would mean I could live together with my mother and my sister again. It was very exciting.

"Hmm. What should I do? What if he comes back and I've already gone? He won't know where to find me."

I sat up in bed and pondered. I couldn't ask Eumis to let him know, because she didn't have my Scarlet Eyes. She wouldn't be able to see him even if he did come back. Besides, he said I was supposed to keep our meeting a secret, and I promised I would.

I wondered and fretted, but in the end, I didn't get anywhere and before I knew it, I had fallen asleep.

A few days later, Eumis came to my room, all smiles.

"Thank you, Shuria," she said. "The spell has finally been completed."

I already knew, because I'd seen the last of my mana leave my body with my Scarlet Eyes. But when that happened, my first thought had been, *Oh, I suppose I'm not going to get to see Kaito again after all.*

"...So does that mean I can go outside again?"

"Yes, you may. I made sure to keep this day open, so why don't we go out together?"

"...I'd like that very much."

"Then it's settled. Soriy, could you get everything ready?"

"Understood, Mistress," replied the maid, bowing and leaving the room.

I would finally get to leave the room and go into town with Eumis. It was like a dream come true.

"This is going to be such a wonderful day," I said.

"Yes, indeed it shall," answered my sister, lips breaking into her usual smile.

After that, I went shopping in town with Eumis. I hadn't had time for sightseeing when I first arrived in the city, and this was my first time seeing it up close.

"Wow, there are so many people and so many shops!"

"Hee-hee! I suppose it must seem that way to you, having lived in a small village for so long."

Eumis was disguised in a low hat and a pair of glasses. I was also wearing a similar hat, but to be honest, it made it a little hard to see, and I didn't like it.

"...Eumis, Eumis, what is that?"

"Oh, that's a magic item for starting fires. We have one at home in the kitchen."

"And what's that?"

"That's a game board."

The warm rays of the sun seemed to be cheering us on as shop-keepers called out their wares in the marketplace. There were more people I could see with a turn of my head than lived in my entire village.

"Ah..."

"What have you found? Oh my, what an adorable doll."

At a stall selling miscellany, I stopped in front of a large stuffed toy of a white kitty cat. It was holding a knife and fork in its hands, and wearing an apron stained with what looked like ketchup.

Eumis looked at me and chuckled. "Excuse me, madam. How much is this doll?"

"That's eight large coppers."

"Thank you very much. Here you go, Shuria."

"…I can have this?"

"Well, it's a bit late to change your mind now, I've already bought it! Hee-hee, here, take it!"

Eumis was very kind. The doll itself was cute, but the fact that my sister bought it and gave it to me made me very happy. I squeezed it tightly and smiled.

"It's almost time for lunch. I've asked Soriy to meet us in the park for sandwiches. Shall we go?"

"Yes, please, Eumis!"

She took me to a wonderful garden. I had read about them in my novels, but never seen one. There was nothing this fancy in the village I was from. We sat on a park bench, eating sandwiches out of a wicker basket.

It wasn't the first time I'd eaten lunch with Eumis, but today was a very special day nonetheless.

After lunch, we went and looked at some more shops. The time flew by, and soon enough, the sky began to redden with the light of dusk.

"Er, Eumis… I had a lot of fun today, but are you sure it didn't bore you?"

"Oh? Why would that be?"

"Well, you had to waste your valuable time off looking after me."

"That isn't true at all. I had fun shopping, too. Besides, today is a very special day, the day the spell of three years in the making finally draws to completion." Eumis smiled. "Now, the sun has almost set. We should go."

"…Go where?"

"Well, the truth is, your mother and sister are already here in this city."

"Huh?!"

"Hee-hee. I knew you'd be surprised, so I kept quiet. Soriy's been helping prepare your welcome-back party, so I expect they're ready waiting for us right now."

Finally... I can see my family again!!

I was very lucky, because Eumis had allowed me to receive letters from them once a month, and visited me herself so I wouldn't be lonely, but it had still been almost three years since I had seen my mother and my sister, so I missed them very much.

"Let's go. They're all waiting for you at your new home."

"Yes!"

Eumis and I set off down the twilit streets. My heart felt like it was going to beat out of my chest. I wanted to run all the way there as fast as I could, but I didn't know the way. Eumis guided me through the unfamiliar city, walking ahead of me.

So I didn't know what kind of face she was making at that moment.

"...This is my new home?"

"Indeed, it is."

Eumis brought me to a quiet building on the outskirts of the city. It was large, but out of the way, and with my Scarlet Eyes, I could see that there were a great number of spells cast on it, just like Eumis's mansion. I didn't have her intuition for magic, so I didn't know what they did, but I thought they must be "defensive wards" of the sort that Eumis had told me about.

"You won't have to worry about Mother and Father. They believe this to be merely one of my research laboratories. Even they cannot enter without my permission."

So even if they came back to the city, we can hide indoors for a few days and they won't find us, I thought. Even though he was my father, I didn't want to see the lord or his wife who had chased us out of the city. I am sure they had no desire to see us, either.

"Let's go inside, shall we?" asked Eumis.

"Yes!"

The inside of the house looked normal. Of course, it was simple compared to my room in Eumis's mansion, but it still looked far more habitable than our village hut.

"Thank you for waiting, Mistress and Miss Shuria."

Soriy bowed her head as she saw us. Wearing her usual maid uniform, she greeted us in a very dignified manner.

But Mother and Shelmie were not with her.

"...Where is my family?"

"They are farther inside," Eumis explained and began walking immediately as though she knew where she was going. She was followed by Soriy, and I trailed after them.

They opened a door I thought would lead to another room of the house, but it appeared to descend into the basement. From below, I could sense an unfamiliar magic I disliked very much.

"Er, Eumis...? Is my family really down here...?"

"This way. Follow me," urged Eumis, and without turning back, she descended the staircase.

"W-wait! Wait for me!"

Feeling uncertain, I followed her down the stairs. With each step, I thought about how I'd soon get to see my family again. I was very excited, but at the same time, a little uneasy.

It was my family. I'd lived with them all my life, and we'd been exchanging letters these past three years. But somehow, I had a strange feeling.

At the base of the stairs was a simple iron door.

"They're both waiting for you, just beyond this door," said Eumis, smiling.

She let me go first. I approached the door and hesitated before it. *Oooh, I'm so nervous.*

What would I say to them first? I wasn't good at being loud, but if there was ever a time to be energetic, this was it. I took a deep breath, pushed open the creaking iron door, and called out in the brightest voice I could manage.

"Mother, Shelmie! It's been so long! I missed...you?"

But I didn't make it to the end of the sentence before my voice failed me.

"..."

What greeted me beyond that door was not what I had expected to see at all.

It was like a prison, as dark and as gloomy as a cave, and the room was full of *things* writhing on the ground, speaking only in strange, groaning sounds. Their bodies were putrid, like animal innards, and their mouths hung open vacantly.

"Eek! Eumis! Those are undead!!"

With my Scarlet Eyes, I could see the negative energy those *things* gave off. It wrapped around them like stagnant murk, the mana I sensed before and found so unpleasant. The *things* looked unlike any creature I had ever seen before, and I couldn't tell what they had originally been, but they were undead, I was sure of it.

"I've never seen these kinds before, but they're undead!"

"That's right, they are. These ones didn't handle the preservation process very well. The mana we used to prevent the flesh from rotting also damaged it and transformed it into that dark color, like filthy ditch water."

"...Huh?"

I looked up at Eumis beside me, but I saw someone else standing there. A stranger, grinning, saying the most peculiar things as if they were perfectly natural.

"Maybe things would be a little different if they still had their hearts, but unfortunately that's just the way it is. Living hearts are absolutely essential for the process of refining magical stones. The undead can go on living without them, but it seems to have deteriorated the body's ability to contain mana and caused the flesh to start rotting."

She placed her hand in her palm and sighed, as though the bizarre sight before me was nothing out of the ordinary at all.

"Wh-what are you saying?"

The person who looked like my sister simply continued to smile.

She had her face, she had her voice, she had her mannerisms.

And yet, I felt like I was looking at someone I had never met before in my life.

"Necromancy is a tricky business. Few are left who practice the arts, and fewer still documents remain. I have failed many times, but these are my most valuable test subjects yet. By sewing together the organs of monsters, I have managed to bring some semblance of life to them. They can even talk, after a fashion, and they never complain about the things I do to them. All that's left now is to find a way to bring back their minds."

"…"

Who was she?

Who was the person standing there, before my eyes?

There's no one I know who makes this face.

There's no one I know who talks like this.

"My, there's no need to look so upset. This is the day you finally get to meet your beloved family again. Smile! They're both watching."

"N-no…"

As I stood there, paralyzed, Eumis took my hand. I tried to pull away, but she was bigger than me.

"It's time for your touching reunion."

"No... What... No... Eumis... Eumis?!"

She threw me into the cell in the back. The kitty doll fell from my hand and tumbled onto the floor. I turned to see her slam the metal door shut with a *clang*.

In that cell with me were those two mysterious undead.

"Eek...!!"

If I looked closely, I could make out their general form. They were like people with no arms or legs. Like the others, these ones had dark, slimy skin, and protrusions where a human would have breasts. On the part most like a head they had no hair, and on their faces there were simply two holes instead of a nose, and a lipless, toothy mouth.

But unlike the others with their hellish groans, these two made no sound at all. They simply watched me through eyeless sockets and crawled slowly closer.

"No...no..."

The previous times I'd encountered the undead I'd had my magic at my side, but now, I had no means to protect myself.

"N-no! Stay away from me! Let me out, Eumis! Let me out!!" I rattled the rusted iron bars of the cell and screamed out in panic at my sister. But all she did was stand there, her smile unbroken.

"Shuria. You always told me you wanted to see a spirit stone."

"Huh? E-Eumis?"

Eumis produced something from her pocket wrapped tightly in cloth. She unwrapped it, and inside was a dark purple stone.

"Th-that mana...it's the same as in my room..."

"Oh, you can tell? Your Scarlet Eyes must really come in handy."

Somehow, my sister's usual smile seemed much wider than normal.

"You should be happy, Shuria. You've always wanted to meet a spirit, haven't you? He's a bit different, but he is still a spirit, technically."

"My, my, how rude. It's been such a long time since I was last summoned, and this is how you treat me?"

A voice came out of nowhere, and mana began to erupt from the stone in Eumis's hand. The same as that emitted by the magic circle in my room, only so thick that even people without my ability would be able to see it. An indescribable color of magic whirled, and a form began to take shape.

"...A demon..."

The figure had a mouth bursting with pointed teeth, a pair of tightly curled goat horns atop his head, wings of jet-black bone and crimson webbing, and ash-black skin, rugged and hard like stone.

Of all the forms demons took in all the writings, this one was the most popular. The *Great Demon*.

While it was indeed a spirit, it was in some ways different. The counterpart to an angel.

"Ah... Uh... Ah..."

What was happening? I could barely make sense of what I was seeing.

"Oh? It was you who told me not to lump you in with the other spirits, was it not?"

"Heh-heh-heh. I can't stand to be treated the same as those bores."

He cackled. It was like a high voice and a low voice all mixed together, and it grated against my ears.

"So this kid's the final sacrifice, is she? Not every day you get to drink elf blood! Hee-hee-hee!"

"N-no... Huh?!"

A long, purple tongue extended from the demon's mouth, dripping with spit. His cross-shaped eyes rattled in their sockets.

"Eumis! Save me! I'm sorry if I did something bad, just make it stop, please!!"

"Oh my, no. You didn't do anything bad, not at all."

She reached her tender hand toward me and softly stroked my cheek.

"This was planned from the start. It's not your fault."

"Huh...?"

"I agreed to hand over your life and soul as part of the conditions for activating the magic circle. He wanted a soul freshly filled with happiness, he said. Isn't that selfish of him?"

"Oh, but I disagree, madam. I am not selfish, I'm a gourmand."

In the flickering light of the candle flame, Eumis's familiar smile looked twisted and warped.

"You demons just say whatever you like. Wasn't it 'quantity over quality' before? That's why we had to destroy her entire village."

"Well, that's just the mood I was in at the time. When there's a lot you don't really care about how they taste. A high-class meal is all well and good, but sometimes you just want to pig out on cheap souls drenched in terror. What is it you humans call it? Ah, yes, 'junk food.'"

"What...are you...talking about...?"

I didn't understand. I didn't understand their words. I didn't understand their actions.

"Well, you know about demons, don't you?" asked Eumis. "They grant you your wishes, but at a high price. He wanted fifty living souls, so I gave him your village. As for the leftovers, I brought them here. Look, can't you see they're welcoming you?"

"Huh?! No...that's not..."

When the meaning of her words finally dawned on me, I looked around at the faces in the room. They looked like nothing born of this earth. They couldn't have been humans at all.

And yet, looking beyond their signature undead mana, I could sense traces of a kind of magic that seemed not unfamiliar to me.

"Huh? That's old man Jass. And that one's Ymir! No... That means...they really are..."

My vision darkened. My ears rang. I felt like I was hearing everything twice.

"Oh wow, you really can tell them apart. Those Scarlet Eyes are going to come in handy. Now then, kill her without damaging the body, as we agreed. You may consume the soul, but everything else belongs to me, and I still have a use for her."

My head was spinning. I reached out my arms, but all I could do was rattle the bars of the iron cage.

"Aaah... Wait...wait! Eumis! Eumiiis!!" I cried, but she turned and walked away, her heels clacking against the stone floor, without once looking back.

Then it was just me and the demon left in that underground prison.

"Ha-ha-ha, I can't believe you'd still cling to that woman after all she's done to you. Still, she is an interesting one, that Eumis. She wasn't put off at all when I devoured her fellow humans before her. Most people at least pale a little, even if they think themselves fit for the role, you know? What a shame she was born as a human and not a demon! Hee-hee-hee!"

"You... You're lying. Eumis would never do that! ...That's right! Mother and Shelmie never mentioned any of this in their letters!"

"Huh? Ahhh, I guess that's true. But only because I didn't order them to."

"...Huh?"

What did he just say?

"Take a closer look at those two undead over there. You can tell, can't you?"

It wasn't possible. It couldn't be true.

Because there was nothing I had done to deserve this...

"Aaah... Aaahhh... Aaaaaaaaaahhhh!!"

"See? Haven't you missed them? Aww, what a lovely scene."

*   *   *

"You finally got to see your old mom and sister again."

As soon as those words reached my ears, my world cracked in half.

"Noooooooooooooo!!"

"Ha-ha-ha-ha-ha-ha!! The smell of despair, as sweet as perfume!"

The mana was faint, but unmistakable. I had seen it every day, in my own home. It belonged to my family.

"Here, since I'm so nice, I'll let 'em talk to you!"

The demon waved his hand, sending his mana into Mother and Shelmie.

"A... Kah..."

"Keh... Grh..."

"Hrh!! Ah...ahhh...ahhh..."

The stiff, clumsy movements of their jaws and the clattering of their teeth eventually settled into the voices I had heard just the other day.

"Shuria, are you well?"

"Have you been well, sister?"

They spoke smoothly, like puppets.

"Stop...please, stop..."

The demon's rough laughter was harsh in my ears. He guffawed as though he were having the time of his life.

"Oh, you must love them ever so much if you can still recognize them. Eee-hee-hee! Isn't it nice you got to see each other again?"

"This can't be real. It can't... Am I a sinner...? Why is this happening to me...?"

"It's real. Real as you and I, princess. If anyone is a sinner, it's that sister of yours. Now ain't she a stinker? It's her who did this to your mom

and sister, you know. Ain't got nothing to do with me. She's a real piece of work, that one! Eee-hee-hee-hee! She's even more devilish than I am!"

My legs buckled out from under me, and I hit the ground. I couldn't even feel the tears on my cheeks anymore.

"…Really."

Everything was topsy-turvy to how I remembered it. The world I thought was made of cotton wool was now a monstrous snare of barbs seeking to entangle and tear me apart.

It was all a lie…from the very beginning. That smile, that kindness. Drinking tea together, discussing books, our outing today, all of it. It was all a lie.

"Ha…ha-ha… What a farce."

How stupid I'd been. I'd thought of her as my sister, while she slaughtered my village and strung me along all this time. She did this to my family, while I sat in that room for three years straight and gave her my power, telling myself it was all to pay her back.

"Oh? Feeling down? Feeling sad, are we?"

"Gr!! Shut up! O ball of raging flame: *Fireball!* …Oh."

My mana leaked feebly out of me without giving form to the spell I wanted.

"Ah… Aaahhh… I can't even cast such a simple spell anymore."

There really was not a single drop of magical ability left in me. There was nothing I could do to the demon before me.

"Hee-hee… Ha-ha! Ha-ha-ha-ha!"

It was like a joke. It was so amusing, I couldn't help it. Bone-dry laughter spilled out of me alongside the tears.

"Hee-hee-hee! Yes, your soul is turning out quite nicely!"

I watched out of the corner of my warped vision as the demon slowly began to unfurl his wings.

"…Why?"

Why did things turn out this way?

How did it come to this?

Just a little while ago, I was the happiest girl in the world. Now, those memories were like needles in my skin.

"Very good. I love a soul seasoned with a bit of grief."

"No more. I don't want to see any more, I don't want to hear any more."

"Yes, you'll do very nicely. Hee-hee-hee! Time to sink my teeth in!"

Even as the color drained from the world, I still saw the twisted smile of the demon. He reached his arms toward me to take my life.

After that, it would all be over. I waited for that moment to come...

...But at the last second, I moved out of the way.

"Hmm? What's this? Still reluctant, are we?"

"...I can't do it. I can't die yet, I just can't... I'll kill her. She'll pay for this! I will have my revenge against her!"

"Good, very good. Now you're talking. You'll taste much better after you've put up a fight!!"

I wanted to live. I couldn't die, couldn't let it be over yet. Even if I had to crawl through the mud, I wouldn't give up. I wanted to kill her, make her suffer, so much I could bear it no longer.

I would destroy her and everything she held dear. If anyone tried to help her, I'd destroy them, too.

"...Stay away from me, demon!!"

"Oh, you wound me, my dear. Boo-hoo."

The detestable fiend before me grinned. If he was going to help her, then so be it.

I'd tear her limb from limb, burn her, bite her, drown her, strangle her.

I just wanted her dead. No, I had to be the one to do it. Be the one to drag her down into a cage of darkness, a darkness unventured by even a single ray of hope.

I scraped up the pebbles by my feet and threw them at him, and when those ran out, I threw sand.

I hated him. I loathed them all! I hated every single thing that put me in this position!

And yet, no matter how hard I rebelled, my unjust end drew closer.

"Grh! Urgh! Ah…!!"

The demon grabbed me by the hair and licked his lips maliciously. He was strong. I couldn't escape.

"Oh, don't worry. I'm not going to leave a mark. I'm just going to stop your heart with my demon poison. It'll only take a second. It won't hurt, honest."

"Y-you…monster! I'll kill you! I swear I will!"

I clawed at his hand with my fingernails, but he didn't react. I wasn't even sure if he felt the pain.

"Ha-ha-ha! How long has it been since I sampled such a delectable soul? Don't worry, you shan't be lonely, I'll send the other two after you to keep you company!"

"Hrh?! No…stop!!"

"Demon Absorb."

The devil stretched his arm out toward mother and Shelmie. He seemed to mutter something, then the bodies underwent what could only be described as an explosion, scattering red human blood all over the place. Then, they dissolved into a black mist and were sucked into his open jaws.

"You…you fiend! How dare you! How dare you!"

"Oh? You're rather feisty all of a sudden. Is it the shock?"

He cackled before me.

"There's no need to be afraid. Soon you'll all be together again… inside my belly!"

The tears ran down my cheeks again, tears of anger and frustration.

Why? How?

They were the only words that came to mind, and I screamed them so hard I thought my throat would tear.

Why were all these bad things happening to me when I hadn't done anything wrong?

"This is too much... It can't end like this..."

I was sure that it wouldn't end with my death, too. She would go on to abuse my body long after, just like she did to Shelmie and Mother. That was what angered me the most.

Where did I go wrong?

When did it all unravel?

Who betrayed me?

"Now then, sit still. It's dinnertime! Eee-hee-hee-hee!!"

I saw in his twisted smile the face of my sister.

"Are you Shuria? Nice to meet you. My name is Eumis. I'm your big sister."

It was the face she'd made when we first met.

Oh, if only I could go back to that day...

"...I'd kill her. I'd kill her for sure."

"Dear lord. I had no idea we were *this* similar. It makes me feel sick."

"Huh...?"

As the iron door of the jail was blasted off its hinges, I heard a familiar voice. It crashed to the ground and a young man strode into the room, with pitch-black hair and opal eyes.

However, he wasn't made of mana this time, but flesh, like a human.

"Kaito...?"

I almost didn't expect him to respond to that name, but the human spoke.

"Hey. Good to see you again, Shuria. Told you we would, didn't I?"

"What's this? Don't you know it's rude to barge in without knocking? Who are you?"

At the demon's question, the man spun around to face him.

"Who am I? Good question. I'd love to say something like, 'If I told you that I'd have to kill you,' but unfortunately I'm here on official business today."

In his hand, he held an azure blade. Two red cords fell from the hilt, adorned with orange cotton wool balls.

"I've come a long way, you know, to kill the woman who summoned you."

A dark, almost heroic grin spread across Kaito's lips. He pointed the tip of his sword at the demon.

"...I'm the stupid Revenant, okay?"

SHORT STORY

An Unrelated Story

An Unrelated Story

Argh, dammit, how did things turn out like this? Today was finally going to be the day I showed those good-for-nothing adventurers my true power, too.

"Haah...haah... Dammit! Why'd we run into Redcaps *here*?!"

"Crap, they keep moving around! Can't land a good hit!"

"Huh. It has been a while since an enemy last dodged my arrows."

...*Huh, these guys are stronger than I imagined*, I thought as I fended off the Redcaps.

The Adventurers Guild had forced me to join Zuily's party for three months as punishment for starting that fight. They didn't give us much choice in the matter. If I refused to work with them, the guild would reject my application, and Zuily's party faced even greater penalties.

If they didn't accept me onto their team and treat me fairly and justly, they would face heavy fines and instant demotion, plus a block on ranking up again for a fixed period. The same if I died or became seriously injured through no fault of my own, though in that case there would be no fine.

I was also prohibited from leaving Zuily's party and taking on requests by myself, and if I fled the town, I'd be banned from the guild for six months.

I was supposed to take the adventuring world by storm! Instead I ended up with a ball and chain around my leg.

And so I had no choice but to get myself comfortable with my new provisional teammates. To start ourselves off, we picked up a quest to slay goblins, something every new adventurer goes through, yet somewhere we ended up in this monster-infested forest, fighting enemies that were never supposed to show up here.

"Daaaaagh?!"

"Keh-keh!!"

Lost in thought, I allowed one of the monsters to get the drop on me. The Redcap's machete only barely scratched my arm, but the cut burned with intense pain. However, I didn't have time to worry about that.

"Grrr, stay back!!" I growled, swinging my staff.

""Keh-keh-keh!""

The two Redcaps slowly drew toward me.

"Keh-keh!!"

"Wha—?!"

I wasn't looking behind me!

Distracted by the two in front, I didn't notice the one sneaking up behind until it was too late.

Is this it? No, I can't die. I don't want to die. Somebody, save me!

"What the hell are you doin'?"

"Gaaaahh!!"

Just before the Redcap's blade reached me, Zuily appeared and sliced the monster in half.

"Haah…haah…haah…"

"Calm down. We can't have you dyin' on us."

"Y-yeah…"

…She saved me. A mongrel of lesser blood saved me. And yet, it was relief I felt, not shame. But I didn't have time to wallow in that feeling, for next Terry hobbled one of the Redcaps with an arrow.

"Geh-geh?!"

"Now!!" he cried.

"Got it," I replied, turning to the spell I had cast so many times before. "O ball of raging flame: *Fireball!*"

"Plergh!!"

The ball of fire leaped from the tip of my staff and engulfed the Redcap in fire.

"*Phew.* Hey, you're pretty good, kid," remarked Dot. "Even takin' that staff o' yours into account. And here I thought it was the one doing all the work."

"An' I thought you'd flub your lines trying to cast that spell," admitted Zuily. "Guess you're not as much of a fraidy-cat as you look."

"H-hmph! Obviously! Don't you know who I am?"

"Enough messing about! They're not all dead yet!"

"Got it!!"

The fight went on. It felt nothing like training alone at home. I felt alive.

Hmph. Well, at least they won't be dragging me down for the next three months.

It didn't take us long to finish off the rest of the Redcaps.

At the beginning, I saw it as a chore. I wished I'd had the sense to cut that argument off before the guild saw fit to intervene.

"Why do we have to babysit? How are we supposed to steal that staff now?"

"Well, ain't no goin' against the guild. What's done is done."

"We just have to wait a few months. Besides, he could be useful if he drops the attitude. We don't have a magic-user in our party, after all."

"Heh. Doubt a posh twat like him has the guts to keep up with us, anyway."

That conversation was only yesterday.

We'd gone to slay goblins as a warm-up, but I didn't expect to be ambushed by Redcaps.

"Haah…haah… Dammit! Why'd we run into Redcaps *here*?!"

My words were filled with frustration. Sure enough, the kid was useless. Just swinging his staff helplessly. But if he died, there's no way we could patch things over with the guild. We'd be penalized for sure.

That's the only reason I jumped in to save him when I saw the Redcap creeping up behind him.

Rrrgh. This sucks. I hate brats who are all talk.

Or so I thought until that moment. Even though he had been on the verge of death, he weaved together his spell perfectly and burned the next Redcap to death.

I was actually impressed, a little. Most people would mess up in a situation like that. And even with his staff helping, he wasn't just barely getting the spell out. He was confident and in control of the magic. In the fight after that, I got to see a little more of his talent.

…I guess I should at least ask his name once the battle is over, I thought, and I continued fighting until all the Redcaps were dead.

After the three months were over, I ended up staying on as a member of Zuily's party. They taught me many things: how to fight monsters, how to avoid danger, how to manipulate people to your advantage, how to force the girl you like to screw you, things of that nature.

They may not have been cut from the same cloth as I, but perhaps when I became a lord, well, maybe I could take them on as my retainers.

I continued journeying with them, and before I knew it, two years had passed. We had dealt with countless requests, and we were now a B-rank party—considered among the best in our field.

We were in the closing moves of the war against the demons: tracking down the demon who called himself the hero. According to our intel, after the hero slew the demon lord, he was tempted by her power and turned over to the side of darkness. With the armies of the world exhausted in battle against the demon lord, the nations put out a collective bounty on the hero's head.

Well, the turning to the dark side thing is probably just a front. I imagine he's simply outlived his usefulness. Still, we can hardly pass this opportunity up.

The ignorant masses probably believed the words of the nations, but I was different. In any case, whether it was true or not hardly mattered. If I could be the one to slay the hero, they'd make me a lord for sure. Perhaps the kingdom would even grant me the hand of the Beauty of Orollea, Princess Alicia. It would just be for show, sure, but it's all the same to me.

While those thoughts preoccupied my mind, I was almost taken by surprise as a garm leaped out of the bushes toward me.

"Grrrrrrrr!! Ruff!"

"Whoops, that was close. *Wind Cutter!*"

A single garm was no match for me now. I sidestepped its claws and let loose a blade of air.

"Gyau…?! Grrr… Ruf…"

"*Tsk.* Got away. It's just a garm, but it's in a demon's territory…"

I definitely hit it, but the garm still scurried away into the trees. I had no time to chase after it.

"Hansel! We've figured out where the hero is hiding! Prepare to begin our assault!"

"Hmm! Got it!"

I tried to still my racing heart. I was finally here. The praise and recognition I was promised was waiting for me just ahead. All I had to do was slay the evil hero. He would be very weak by now.

"I wonder what I should do when I become king...," I pondered aloud, smiling as I made my way alone through the forest.

The Hero Laughs While Walking the Path of VENGEANCE a Second Time

NERO KIZUKA
Illustration by SINSORA

"Vengeance upon vengeance."

VOLUME 3 COMING SOON!